# DANGEROUS TEXAS HIDEOUT

## VIRGINIA VAUGHAN

**LOVE INSPIRED** SUSPENSE

INSPIRATIONAL ROMANCE

# LOVE INSPIRED® SUSPENSE
### INSPIRATIONAL ROMANCE

Recycling programs
for this product may
not exist in your area.

ISBN-13: 978-1-335-59787-8

Dangerous Texas Hideout

Copyright © 2024 by Virginia Vaughan

For questions and comments about the quality of this book, please contact us
at CustomerService@Harlequin.com.

Love Inspired
22 Adelaide St. West, 41st Floor
Toronto, Ontario M5H 4E3, Canada
www.LoveInspired.com

Printed in U.S.A.

What time I am afraid, I will trust in thee.
—*Psalm* 56:3

# ONE

Penny Jackson gripped her daughter Missy's hand as they stepped out of the grocery store and into the humid Texas afternoon. She scanned the parking lot for any hint of danger, as had become her custom anytime they ventured outside since fleeing their Kentucky home sixty-seven days ago. She'd stayed away from town as long as she could, but they'd been out of food and necessities, so she'd finally had to take a trip to the grocery store to resupply.

Cars and people came and went but nothing stood out to her. Seeing no obvious threat, she gripped the child's hand and hurried across the walkway to where she'd parked her car. A man passed in front of her, tipped his cowboy hat and smiled. He was tall with a strong jaw and green eyes that might have made her smile back a few weeks ago, pleased at the attention. Today, she gulped hard before acknowledging him with nothing more than a nod, then quickly moved past him. He was wearing a police uniform and the last thing she needed was police involvement.

She'd had enough of that with the FBI and Marshals.

None of them had been looking out for her daughter. They'd only been looking to capture and bring down a bank robbery ring no matter the cost.

She fumbled for her keys, balancing groceries and a fidgety six-year-old child. Missy was restless and edgy. She had good reason to be. They both did. But Penny wasn't going to let anything happen to her daughter. She clicked the button on her key fob, then loaded the groceries into the cargo space of her SUV. Missy jumped and played until Penny, irritated, raised her voice and told the girl to settle down and be still. It wasn't fair that Missy didn't get the exercise she needed and Penny knew she shouldn't take her frustration out on her daughter when she had so much energy to burn, but their situation was beginning to take a toll.

She closed the tailgate, then grabbed Missy's hand again and pushed her shopping cart to the return corral. The sooner they were back in the safety of their rented home, the better she would feel. She would let Missy run around the living room to her heart's content and not complain one time.

They were heading back to the SUV when tires squealed nearby. Penny looked to her right and saw a car roaring toward them. The sun glared off the windshield, making her unable to see the driver's face. Fear paralyzed her. This couldn't be happening again. It couldn't.

Missy cried out and Penny instinctively held her close.

Suddenly, strong arms grabbed them both and pulled them to the ground as the car roared by, barely missing them.

She looked up into kind, deep green eyes and a worried expression. The policeman who'd smiled at her earlier. "Are you both okay?"

Missy whimpered and tears filled her eyes. Penny glanced down and saw she was holding her knee. She'd scraped it when they'd tumbled.

"Hey, I'm sure it hurts, but that looks like it's going to be okay," the man said to Missy. "We'll find you a Band-Aid." He turned to Penny. "What about you? Are you injured?"

She shook her head. "I—I'm okay." Her face flushed. She hated all the lying. Physically, she was unharmed—except maybe a scraped palm or knee like Missy—but emotionally, she was a wreck. Someone had targeted her and Missy.

Again.

"My name is Caleb. I'm the chief of police here in Jessup. You've had a close call. It's okay to be a little shaken but you're safe now."

*Oh, how she wished that were true.*

"I—I think we're okay, officer."

His mouth turned up on one side. "Caleb, please."

She allowed him to help her to her feet, ignoring the flutter in her stomach that had more to do with the man who'd swooped in and saved them than it did their near miss. She turned and quickly checked Missy over. She seemed to be uninjured except for the scrape, but she was scared and with good reason.

Caleb pulled a radio from his belt and clicked on it. "This is Chief Harmon. Send a team to Walker's Grocery. We have a near hit-and-run. Also, put out a BOLO on a silver Nissan Sentra. The driver nearly ran down a woman and her child, then kept going." He rattled off the tag number then turned to Penny. "Do either of you need to go to the hospital?"

The hospital was the last thing they needed. They would ask too many questions she didn't feel safe answering. "No, we're fine. I'd just like to go home now. I've got frozen foods defrosting."

It was as good an excuse as any and not a lie. In the Texas heat, her refrigerated items would be spoiled soon.

He glanced toward her vehicle, then back at her. "I really have to get your statement about what happened. We need to catch up to that driver and cite him for at least reckless driving. Did you recognize him or the car?"

She shook her head. "I didn't—or at least, the car isn't familiar, and I couldn't see the driver well enough to tell if he looked familiar or not. I was returning my cart to the corral. The sun was glaring off the windshield. He likely didn't see me either." At least, she hoped that was the case. It would be much better than the alternative—that they'd been discovered by the men chasing after them.

"That's still no excuse for going as fast as he was through this area."

His face was full of indignation. He was getting involved and the last thing she needed was for him to pay any extra attention to them.

"Don't worry about it, Chief. We're unharmed and we really just want to get home."

He hesitated before finally acquiescing. "Fine but

give me your name and number in case I need to follow up with you."

She didn't want to give him that information but how could she get away with refusing? She reluctantly told him. "My name is Penny Anderson," she said, giving him the false name she'd come up with. "This is my daughter, Missy."

He knelt down. "Nice to meet you, Missy." He held out his hand to her but she quickly moved behind Penny's leg.

"She's very shy," Penny explained. She didn't add that she hadn't always been this way or that she no longer spoke a word…not since the incident that had sent them running.

Thankfully, he didn't ask questions about her daughter's lack of social skills but it made Penny's heart ache to remember a time when Missy would have peppered him with a hundred different questions instead of hiding behind her.

He stood and pulled out his notebook. "That's okay. I guess I can be pretty scary, can't I?"

She smiled at his attempt at humor. They knew scary and he wasn't it.

"Your address and phone number?"

She gave him the number to the prepaid cell she'd purchased when she and Missy had fled Kentucky two months ago.

Now this had happened.

She'd let down her guard and come out into the open. Had the killer been waiting for her?

She shuddered and, to her horror, Caleb noticed.

"Are you sure you're okay?" He reached out his hand and touched her arm. For a moment, she wondered what it would be like to be wrapped in his arms. It had been too long since anyone had offered her comfort or reassurance and she needed it.

But she couldn't give in to it. Not when her daughter's life was at stake. "I'm fine, but I really need to go." She walked to the SUV and loaded Missy into the car seat. They had to get out of here.

"I'll call you if I need anything else," Caleb said.

She nodded, then slipped behind the steering wheel. Getting home was her top priority. Getting Missy to safety.

She quickly started the engine and drove away before Chief of Police Caleb Harmon could ask her any more questions or stretch her reserve any further.

The incident at the grocery store was still bothering Caleb a short while later when he made it back to the police station.

Seeing a pretty lady in town shouldn't send up red flags but it had. Jessup wasn't exactly a mecca of tourism. They were just a small town that got few visitors. She wasn't the first out-of-towner he'd come across, but her demeanor had piqued his interest. He could see something was out of the ordinary the moment she'd flashed him a terrified smile as he'd passed her by on his way into Walker's.

Then the car nearly running her down. Red flag number two.

Something just seemed off about the whole situation, though he struggled to put his finger on what had him uneasy. Maybe it was the fact that Penny Anderson hadn't showed the appropriate outrage at nearly being hit by a car and nearly having her daughter hit too. Most people would have been calling for the driver's head, but her main concern had been to get out of there.

He rubbed his jaw. He was probably overthinking it. She'd had a trauma, and everyone responded to that differently. She'd seemed worried about her daughter, which was natural enough. Maybe she just wasn't the confrontational type and had been more focused on getting the girl safely home. There wasn't anything suspicious about that—on the surface, anyway. But fourteen years of law enforcement and his gut told him something was off about the whole situation.

He checked in with Hansen, the officer on duty. "Anything pressing?"

"No, it's a quiet day except for your call. What happened there?"

"A woman and her daughter were crossing the street when a car nearly ran them down. Didn't look like he slowed down at all either. The guy was probably on his phone and not paying attention." At least he was hoping that the explanation was that innocent, but Penny Anderson's reaction screamed at him that something more was going on. "Any movement on the BOLO?"

"Nothing so far."

"What about the license plate numbers I gave you?" He hadn't been able to help himself. He'd jotted down her plate number along with that of the sedan and texted them to Hansen after she'd left the scene.

Hansen turned to the computer and pulled up a report. "One came back to a Charles Morton. Forty-three. No tickets or citations on file."

"And the other?"

He pressed a button and another report appeared on screen. "Penny Jackson. Twenty-nine. A Lexington, Kentucky address."

His heart sank. Just as he'd suspected. She'd been lying to him. "She told me her name was Penny Anderson."

The fact that she'd given him a false name along with her odd behavior sent a third red flag up for him. He knew a woman who was running when he saw one. "Did you check for criminal backgrounds?"

"Nothing on Mr. Morton. He's clean. Looks like she's wanted for questioning by the FBI in connection to a string of bank robberies."

Bank robberies?

If she was a wanted woman, it would explain her squirrelly behavior and her rush to get away from him. But instead of feeling like he finally had the answer, he was just left with more questions. He generally trusted his instincts and they were lit up now, letting him know that something about this woman wasn't adding up. While her behavior at the scene had seemed inappropriate to the situation, she certainly hadn't seemed like a bank robber. She'd almost seemed more scared than angry. Was someone after her? Was she hiding from someone? Even if she was a thief, maybe she'd been pressured or coerced into it—perhaps by the person she was now running from.

"You want me to respond to the BOLO, Chief?"

"No, I'll take care of it." Hansen handed him a sticky note with the FBI contact info written on it. "See if you can find out more about that BOLO," he instructed Hansen. "I want to know what exactly her involvement is."

He walked into his office and shut the door. He placed his cowboy hat on the desk and fell into his chair, still struggling to get a handle on the woman he couldn't seem to get out of his head.

Obviously, she was on the run from something but, despite the BOLO, he doubted she was a bank robber. She just didn't strike him as the type. A girlfriend of one of them maybe or a material witness.

He rubbed his face as the plight of this mom and her child got under his skin.

He stared at the sticky note with the FBI information..He wanted to know more about what was going on with her.


Penny prepared chicken nuggets and apple slices for Missy for supper. It wasn't as nutritious a meal as she would have preferred but Missy enjoyed it and cleared her plate for a change. Her appetite hadn't been the best since the incident so Penny had tried to cater to what she would eat. It was bad enough that the girl had retreated into a shell and wasn't speaking. She couldn't handle Missy not eating too.

She watched her daughter on the floor, coloring a picture, and her heart ached to go back to their lives before that day at the bank, before they'd been caught up in a robbery. She would never forgive herself for being in that place at the wrong time. Ever since, she'd spent hours trying to figure out what she'd done wrong, how she could make sure something like that never happened again. Of course she hadn't been able to find any solutions. There was nothing she could have done. She hadn't known about the robbery or what would happen. But now she had to live with its aftermath—and so did her daughter. Missy had watched it all unfold, her childhood innocence lost in the blink of eye.

All the bank robbers had been wearing masks but from her vantage point, Missy had been able to see two of their faces without them realizing it. She'd picked them out from their mug shots to the police, showing incredible courage despite struggling with her own fears. Afterward, when everyone realized Missy could identify the men who'd robbed the bank, the threatening notes and harassing phone calls had begun.

Penny had hoped that making it clear that her daughter was not testifying would mean that the threats would end, but they'd only escalated until their FBI protection detail had been murdered in the hotel where they were hiding. After that, Penny had made the decision to slip past their guards and disappear. She'd gotten into her car and driven from Lexington, not even knowing where she was heading but determined to get out of town as fast as possible, away from the men who were targeting them—and also from the police and FBI trying to bully her daughter into testifying no matter the cost. That had been two months ago. Sixty-seven days of peace from the threats and harassment.

She'd done what she had to do to keep her daughter safe.

She only wished she'd been able to get Missy the emotional help she needed.

She sighed. No use fretting over that. There was nothing she could do to change the situation. They'd had no choice but to run. She was determined to get Missy counseling just as soon as it was safe enough to go out in public again. If today had proved anything to her, it was that laying low for now was their safest option.

She helped Missy clean up her colors and papers before bedtime. The current drawing she was working on showed images of people lying on the ground, blood spatter everywhere and an angry man with a gun. Penny shuddered and folded it. Another one for the collection. Missy's drawings since that day at the bank had gotten darker and darker.

She put Missy to bed, kissed her good-night, then walked back into the small living room of their rental. She fell onto the couch and let the tears flow. She needed the release. They were in way over their heads already. Piling the stress of the incident today on top of that was almost too much to comprehend. Part of her had been so fearful that they'd been discovered that she'd wanted to keep driving away from Jessup the moment she'd left the grocery store, but she'd calmed down and convinced herself that it had been nothing more than what the chief had said. A reckless driver who hadn't been paying attention.

She clung to that notion. Carelessness, she could deal with. The thought of it being deliberate malice—the same cruelty that had dogged their footsteps before— was more than she could take.

*God, I can't do this anymore. I need to keep Missy safe but I'm afraid.*

She hadn't meant to invoke God's name in her anguished cry. God used to be her comfort and her guide, but ever since she'd found herself a single mom, God had seemed so distant. Her husband, Devon, had been killed in a bar fight. He and another man had fought over money and drugs, and the fight had turned lethal. She'd been aware of Devon's issues and she'd done her best to help him pay the bills and be supportive, but the lying and the late nights and the drinking had all taken their toll. He'd proved to her that not everyone was who they seemed. If she couldn't even trust her own husband, then who could she trust? In the time since then, she'd learned to rely solely on herself. That attitude had given her independence…but it had also left her lonely. And now, when she really needed someone on her and Missy's side, she had no one to turn to.

Especially not God, who seemed to have turned His back on them.

She got up and dragged herself to her bed, shut off the light and did her best to get some sleep. Being always on guard was exhausting.

A noise pulled her awake. She had no idea how long she'd been asleep but it was still dark outside.

She jerked up in bed, straining to hear again whatever it was that had awakened her.

She pushed back the blanket and slipped into her shoes, which she kept ready and waiting beside the bed.

She slipped her cell phone into her purse and slid the strap over her head. Being ready to move at the drop of a hat was a necessity she'd gotten used to.

Her heart kicked up a notch as she heard something else. It sounded like voices outside.

She darted from her bed and ran into her daughter's room. She pulled back the blankets, thankful for once for Missy's lack of speaking. She groaned and clung to Penny but she didn't cry out. "Baby, we've got to go," Penny whispered to her.

She walked to the bedroom door and opened it slightly to hear if they'd entered the house. The sound of footsteps on the wooden deck out back sent her heart racing.

There was no more waiting around. Someone was coming inside the house.

She opened Missy's bedroom window and peeked through to make sure no one was in range to see them. When she was certain the coast was clear, she pushed it all the way open and crawled through with Missy in her arms just as she heard glass breaking at the back of the house.

She darted toward her car, digging for her keys which she always kept close at hand along with her phone. She climbed inside and started the engine, before roaring away. "Buckle yourself into your car seat," she commanded her daughter who did as she asked.

Penny glanced in the rearview mirror and spotted two men running down her driveway.

Fear lit inside her. She hadn't been imagining it. They'd found them. If she couldn't outrun them now, they would overpower her until she and Missy were both dead.

She had no idea which direction she was driving but she hit the closest highway and floored it. She thought momentarily about calling the police. That might help to slow down the men after her, but it would also mean having to remain in town to explain what was going on. She wouldn't put Missy at risk that way. Especially when she couldn't count on those in authority to have her and her daughter's best interests at heart. She wouldn't allow another set of law enforcement officials to lecture her about how Missy's testimony was all that mattered—not her peace of mind or her safety.

The memory of meeting Caleb struck her. He was the chief of police and seemed like a good man. But could she really trust him? Again, she had to think of Missy. She couldn't stop for anyone, not when her daughter's life depended on it.

Headlights in her rearview mirror told her that it was already too late. The men who'd broken into her house had followed her. It had to be them, given how fast they were driving. It would only be a matter of moments before their vehicle caught up with her.

That did it. She still wasn't sure she could trust the police…but desperate times called for desperate measures. If calling in the authorities was the only way to protect her daughter from certain death right here and now, then she'd do exactly that. At this point, she'd take any help she could get.

She grabbed her phone and dialed 911. "Please help me," she cried when the dispatcher answered. "Two men in a pickup truck are following me. I'm on Route 17 just past the abandoned gas station. They broke into my house. I think they're going to hurt us. My six-year-old daughter is in the car with me."

"Ma'am, hang on," the dispatcher replied. "We have officers responding to your location. Can you see the men?"

"They're right behind me, coming up fast."

"Don't stop. Just keep driving. My officers will find you."

Suddenly, the truck pulled up beside her. She looked over and saw a man lean out the window with a rifle. Missy screamed from the back seat and she knew the police were not going to make it to her in time.

They were on their own.

She sped up and tried to avoid them but the truck managed to keep up with her. Her car didn't have the power their pickup did. The guy fired just as she swerved, shooting out the back seat window.

"Missy!" she screamed, relieved to hear the girl cry out in response. She was frightened and crying but she was alive—for now.

The truck swerved into her lane, shoving the front end of her car. Penny lost control as the car skidded onto the shoulder, then flipped again and again down the steep embankment before sliding to a stop.

Pain riddled through her and her ears were still ringing from the gun blast. Her head hurt and her muscles ached but she managed to unbuckle herself and climb into the back seat to unbuckle Missy. The girl's cheeks were red and wet and she had a few small cuts on her hands, but otherwise she seemed unhurt from the crash.

"We're okay, baby," she said, doing her best to soothe Missy. "We're okay."

She heard movement outside the car and knew the two assailants were coming after them to finish the job. She scrambled to find her purse, then dug into it until her hand clutched the gun inside. She'd hoped to never need it. It had belonged to Devon, and Penny had never fired it, had never even touched it until this mess with Missy had started. But she'd looked up online how to use it. She knew what to do. She felt certain that if it came down to protecting her daughter, she wouldn't hesitate.

She whispered for Missy to get behind her and she did, clinging to Penny's back. The ringing in her ears was beginning to clear and she heard footsteps approaching their vehicle. Penny and Missy were trapped inside, unable to get past whomever was out there.

She raised the gun at the open window.

This was it. It would come down to this. She would fight to the death to save her daughter.

# TWO

Caleb turned on his lights and sirens as he approached the scene. He'd been close by, having recently driven by the house to make sure everything was okay. Everything had seemed quiet and peaceful then, but something had obviously happened soon after he'd left the vicinity.

He spotted two men—apparently spooked by the siren—scrambling back up the embankment to the pickup parked on the shoulder of the road. Pulling over, he saw an overturned SUV at the bottom. He snapped a photo from his phone of the pickup as it sped away. He would deal with them later. First, he needed to find out if the people in the SUV were safe.

He called it in as he hurried down the embankment to the overturned vehicle. He recognized it as the one Penny Anderson—aka Penny Jackson—had been driving earlier that afternoon. "Hello? Is anyone hurt in there?" He knelt so he could see into the car and was instantly met with a gun to his face.

He jerked backward, startled, then slowly inched his way back so he could see Penny and she could see his face. He raised his hands so she could see he was no threat to her. "It's just me, Caleb Harmon. The police chief. We met earlier today."

Even in the little light available, he could see her hands shaking with fear.

"I just want to know you both are okay," he stated, keeping his tone as calm as possible.

"Those men… Where are they?" The tremor of fear in her voice struck him. There was no doubt she was scared. The dispatcher had played the 911 call for him on his way to the scene.

"A truck sped away as I pulled up. Were they chasing you?"

She nodded. "They broke into my house. After we snuck out a window and got to my car, they chased us and ran us off the road."

"They're gone now. It's just me but I've got other officers responding to the call. I should warn you, they won't react as calmly as I am to having a gun pulled on them."

She seemed to consider his statement but didn't lower her weapon.

He tried again. "Penny, please put the gun away. You're safe now. I promise." A memory of saying that to her earlier struck him. She'd looked doubtful then and she'd been right. She and her daughter were obviously not safe.

But despite her clearly justified fear, she *did* seem to be listening to him. Slowly, she lowered the gun and he didn't take a breath until it was on the roof of the overturned car.

"Good. Can you get out of the car on your own or do you need help?"

She shook her head. "We're okay." She turned to her daughter and took her arm, helping her crawl out. Caleb grabbed hold of the child as she exited and moved her out of the way so he could help her mother.

"Stay right here," he told the little girl.

Sirens in the distance indicated his backup was on the way. He was concerned that if he hadn't been close by, the assailants might have killed them before help could arrive.

He hurried back to the car and helped Penny to her feet as she crawled out of the overturned vehicle. Blood dripped down from a cut on her face but she was steady on her feet and nothing appeared to be broken. From looking at the condition of the car, it amazed him that neither of them were seriously injured.

"Let's go. I'll help you back up the hill." He held on to her arm as they climbed the embankment, stopping only a moment for her to take the girl's hand.

Assistance arrived as they reached the road. An ambulance sped to a stop and two paramedics he knew and trusted hopped out.

"There are no obvious injuries but I'll let you take it from here," he said, handing over their care to the EMTs.

He turned to Penny. In the harsh, flashing red-and-blue lights, she looked even more fragile. "This is Jason," he said pointing to the paramedic. "He and his partner, Kevin, are going to take care of you and Missy. I'll be right here if you need me. Okay?"

She nodded. Even though he hated to leave her, he needed to update his team about the situation.

He walked over to his officers who'd arrived on the scene. "A truck sped away as I pulled up. The lady claims two men broke into her house, then chased them down and ran them off the road. I'm sending you all a photo I took of the vehicle as it sped away. We need to put a BOLO on it right away. I want to find the men responsible for this."

His officers got to work processing the scene while he headed back to the ambulance to check on Penny and Missy. It was time to get some answers from her.

"How are we doing?" Caleb asked as he approached the back of the ambulance. Penny and her daughter were sitting inside it on a gurney. Jason had bandaged the gash on Penny's forehead while Kevin had wrapped a few cuts on the little girl's hands and bandaged her arm. She was clutching a stuffed animal—it looked to be a sock monkey—against her chest and looked on the verge of crying at any moment, her wide brown eyes frightened and weary.

The little girl moved closer to her mother who placed her arm around her shoulder before answering Caleb's question.

"Physically, we're okay. I just don't know what we're going to do now."

Jason spoke up. "I only sees cuts and bruises and neither claims to have lost consciousness but I think they both should get checked out at the hospital."

"I need to get your official statement of what happened. I'd also like to return to your house and check it out if you'll allow me. You said the two men broke in?"

She nodded. "Missy and I were both sleeping but I heard something. It woke me up. When I realized they were about to come inside the house, I grabbed her and ran to the car. They chased after us."

The fact that they'd chased them didn't sit well with him. It certainly wasn't normal behavior for burglars to follow their victims out of the house and try to run them down.

More and more, he was convinced there was something else going on.

"Did you know these two men?"

She shook her head. "I didn't get a great look at them but I don't think I've ever seen them before."

"Why do you think they chased you?"

"I don't know." Her demeanor said she did but she wasn't ready to give that information up yet. Whatever she was hiding was probably tied to this break-in.

"May I have permission to check out your house?"

She nodded. "Fine."

"I'll go look and see if there's any damage or anything obvious missing. I'll meet you and your daughter at the hospital afterward."

She glanced at her vehicle and tears filled her eyes. "It's totaled, isn't it?"

"Most likely."

"What are we going to do now?" The helplessness in her whispered question told him she wasn't really asking his opinion.

Losing a vehicle was bad but not as bad as losing

their lives. "Cars can be replaced. You and your daughter can't. We'll figure it out. I'll see you at the hospital."

He closed the ambulance doors and it sped away, carrying them off.

He had an officer retrieve the keys from the ignition of the crashed SUV. "Finish processing the scene. I'll see you back at the office." He slid into his vehicle and drove to her house, parking on the curb.

Turned out, he didn't need the key to get inside. The front door was standing open when he arrived. He pulled his gun and stepped inside, scanning the small living room and kitchen. Whoever those men had been, they might have returned—or perhaps there had been more than two of them and one had stayed behind. The back door lock was broken, indicating they'd forced their way inside, but he spotted no obvious signs that they'd been searching for anything to steal. The small TV still sat in the corner but he didn't see much else of value to be taken in the first place. Was that because they'd already taken it? But there weren't any obvious empty spaces or loose plugs to indicate that there were more electronics that had been taken. And there were no drawers pulled out or furniture overturned the way he'd expect if thieves had tossed the place, looking for hidden valuables. Maybe nothing had been taken because it hadn't been valuables that they'd been after?

He cleared the house and found no one inside. They hadn't come back, and if anyone had been left behind, they'd already made their exit. The door had likely been left ajar when they'd rushed out after Penny and Missy.

Everything indicated that this was more than a simple break-in.

He saw some drawings on the coffee table and picked one up. It was obviously drawn by a child but the colors of red and black were prominently featured. From what he could tell, it looked like a drawing of someone dead on the ground with blood gushing from him and a man standing over him with a gun.

He shuddered at the image and more so at the idea that that sweet little girl he'd met today had drawn something so ugly. She must have witnessed something terribly violent in order to be able to draw it so vividly.

He glanced down and pushed papers aside, finding several more equally disturbing pictures. No one who'd seen these would believe this girl was emotionally okay. Enough was enough. He was ready to find answers and Penny Jackson was going to give them to him.

He arranged for a team to come and collect fingerprints and other trace evidence at the house. Perhaps these men had left a fingerprint or shoeprint or something else behind that they could use to identify them. He secured the back door while waiting for the team to arrive, then instructed them to lock up once they'd finished. Afterward, he headed to the hospital.

Penny was sitting on a gurney beside her daughter who was getting stitches for a cut on her arm.

"Everything okay?"

"Yes, she cut her arm during the crash. It only needed a few stitches. Then she'll be all good," the doctor insisted. He smiled at the little girl who didn't smile back and continued to cling to her mother.

Caleb was beginning to understand this pair better. Based on those drawings he'd seen, they'd been witnesses to something violent and were obviously hiding out from the aftermath of it.

Once the doctor finished and left, Caleb pulled the nurse who remained aside. "Do you think you could take Missy out of here so I can talk to her mother for a few minutes?"

Penny resisted. "I'd rather she stay with me."

Her mama-bear protectiveness was on full display but Caleb thought it was best not to traumatize the child anymore.

"I'll take her out to the vending machine," the nurse, a woman with a big smile and a name tag that read *Rhonda*, stated. "Would you like to get a drink?"

The little girl nodded, then looked at her mother.

"We'll be right outside the door," Rhonda insisted.

Finally, Penny relented and the nurse took the girl's hand and walked out, closing the door behind them.

"There were definite signs that someone was inside your house. The door was left standing open and there was broken glass by the back door. It looks like that's where they entered. I sent a team over to try to gather forensic evidence. Hopefully, they'll give us a lead on who these men are." He pulled one of the drawings he'd found on the coffee table from his pocket and unfolded it. "I also found this."

She stared at the picture her child had drawn and tears filled her eyes but she didn't explain.

"Based on this, I'd say you two have been through something and are probably hiding out here in town.

If that's the case, I'd say you likely know the men who broke into your house, then ran you off the road. Tell me who did this to you and let me help you."

She shook her head. "I have no idea who they were."

Based on her expression and the anxious tone in her voice, he didn't think that was exactly the truth but he felt it wasn't completely a lie either. "But you know why they were there, don't you?"

She hopped off the gurney, leaving the picture lying there. She looked away from him and folded her arms over her chest. She was definitely hiding something and on the run, fleeing from someone. What could she have gotten involved in that would have resulted in a violent scene like the one Missy had drawn? Had there been an abusive spouse or boyfriend who'd attacked someone for getting too close to them? Had someone in their life gotten involved in drugs—and maybe had a drug deal go wrong? Based on the BOLO from the FBI, she had some connection to a robbery. Had her boyfriend or husband been one of the bank robbers?

He lowered his voice as he approached her. "You can trust me, Penny."

"Why?" She spun around and tears welled in her eyes. "Why can I trust you? You can't help me. You can't keep us safe. No one can."

"Maybe I can. At least let me try."

"I've heard those promises before and they're empty. All you people care about is getting what you want."

"And what do I want?"

She stared at him. "I don't know what you want specifically, but I won't allow you to use me or my daughter in order to get it. I have to think about her safety first. I can't risk that for anything."

He pulled his hand through his hair, frustrated. Someone already had her good and scared. He needed to try a different tactic. "I don't want anything from you, Penny. I can see you and your daughter are in some kind of trouble and I want to help you if I can. That's all."

"The only help I need is getting another vehicle so I can get out of this town before those men come back."

"And what then? Keep running? Spend your daughter's whole life running?"

Her face hardened. "It's better than the alternative."

"Which is what?" Still, she hesitated. "Think about your daughter. Something is troubling her." He picked up the drawing. "This…this isn't normal."

She snatched it from him. "I know it's not."

"She needs to see someone. Whatever happened to her, to both of you… She's obviously having trouble dealing with it."

She sighed as a tear slid down her cheek. She brushed it away and admitted, "We were supposed to see a child psychologist. I had the appointment but then…" She shrugged and didn't finish her thought.

But he needed to know. "Then what?"

"Someone broke into the hotel where we were staying. He shot the agent who was protecting us. Missy and I were hiding in the closet. Apparently, the agent had called for backup and they arrived before he found us. They scared him off for the moment, but I knew then they couldn't keep us safe. I got into my car and just drove as fast as I could."

He was confused. Was she talking about what had just happened? "Tonight? That's what happened tonight?" But how could that be? No one had been shot at her house. There were no signs of assault at all.

She shook her head. "Two months ago. Sixty-seven days to be precise. We've been hiding out ever since."

So they were on the run. But why?

"Penny, why did those men attack you?"

"Missy and I were caught inside a bank while it was being robbed. The robbers all wore masks, but Missy was hiding under a desk and she saw two of them when they let down their guard and lowered their masks. She could identify their faces. She even pointed them out to the police through their mug shots. Based on her identification, they tied three other men to a multistate bank robbery ring. The FBI were ecstatic. She was the star witness they'd been waiting for. They promised to protect us, but they couldn't. There were threatening phone calls and notes and someone vandalized my apartment. They even sent me a photograph of Missy at school, overlaid with the image of a rifle scope. Her head was right in the bull's-eye. After that, I changed my mind about letting her stay involved in the case. I said she wouldn't testify, but the FBI agent in charge kept pressing me. She said the men wouldn't stop coming after Missy even if she didn't testify—because there was always a chance she'd change her mind and testify later. She said they had to get rid of Missy to silence her permanently, and that the only way to protect her would be to make sure they were convicted. She put us up at a hotel and had another agent standing guard. It didn't

help. Someone broke in. The intruder shot the agent."
She wiped a tear from her eye. "That's when she stopped
speaking. I knew. I knew I couldn't let anything else
happen to her. I thought if we left, if we refused to testify and disappeared, they would leave us alone. But it
seems the agent was right. They came after us anyway."

So that was their story. They were on the run from
the men who were trying to stop her daughter from testifying against them, men who had no qualms about
murdering a federal agent.

Bank robbers were notoriously pack driven. If one was
arrested, the others would either scatter or close ranks.

He stared out the door at the little girl and thought
about how terrified she must have been. He rubbed his
face, understanding how important she was to putting
a group of bad men in prison. But in the agent's zeal
to close this case, who had been looking out for that
little girl?

He looked back at Penny and realized she'd turned
her world upside down in order to try to keep her daughter safe. What kind of a mother did that? A good one
obviously.

"What about witness protection? Did they offer you
that?"

"They were working on that when the agent protecting us was killed. Don't you understand? These men
found us while we were under federal protection. And
anyway, that's not an option now. I've already told you
I'm not going to let her testify, and we're not eligible
for witness protection unless she does. I can't risk her
life that way."

She seemed stubbornly set on that and he bit back the urge to remind her that their lives already were in danger. "Why don't I take you both back to your house? I'll make sure it's secure and I'll leave an officer to guard it. You'll be safe there. If those men return, we'll capture them." It was a risk taking them back to the house when the bad guys definitely knew its location, but with an officer standing guard and his team on alert, it was their best option. He didn't know where these men were hiding out and taking them both into the open again would be even riskier.

She looked ready to flee and he suspected that had been exactly what she'd be doing if her car hadn't been totaled. But now, she had no means of escape. Finally, after probably working through numerous plans in her mind, she acquiesced. "Thank you. I would feel better at home."

*Right, give her another night to plan her escape and they'll be gone by morning.* Well, he wasn't going to let that happen. These two needed help and he was going to give it.

She opened the door where Missy and the nurse were waiting. She knelt and pulled Missy into a hug. He could see how important her child was to her and he admired her tenacity to protect her.

What would his own mother have done in this situation?

He pushed that random thought aside. It didn't apply here. His mother hadn't been in anywhere near as dire straits as Penny and she'd still left him. If his life had been in danger, she still would have done just what she had done—rescued herself from a life of single motherhood.

He drove them back to their house, then cleared it again to make sure no one had entered while he was away. The crime scene crew had come and gone and they'd done a good job of not leaving a mess behind. He was thankful for that at least.

He watched as Missy bounded into the living room and to the coffee table, picked up her crayons and started drawing again. He couldn't see what she was drawing but based on the other pictures he had seen, it couldn't be good. She should be drawing houses and puppy dogs and rainbows, not blood and death.

She needed help to deal with the trauma she'd witnessed and the only way she was going to get that was if she and her mother got somewhere where they didn't have to look over their shoulders all the time.

He double-checked the locks, then made certain one of his officers was parked on the curb in front of her house. Having a noticeable police presence would alert the bad guys that they couldn't sneak in and get to Penny and Missy.

He turned to leave but Penny stopped him at the door by touching his arm. Her touch sent sparks through him.

But it was her lovely brown eyes staring up at him that pulled at his heartstrings. "Thank you for your help, Caleb."

He smiled. That was the first time she'd said his name and it felt like a step in the right direction. "You're welcome. My only concern here is to make sure you and Missy are safe." He jotted down his cell phone number and handed it to her. "If there's an emergency, call 9-1-1. But if there's anything else, that's my direct line. If you need me, call."

"I will."

He didn't want to leave but sensed it was time to go. He called goodbye to Missy, who ignored him, then said his good-night to Penny before walking out. He heard the locks engage the moment the door shut. Good.

He gave final instructions to the officer on duty to watch the place closely and alert him if he spotted anyone or anything suspicious. Then he climbed into his car and headed back to the police station. He wanted to learn everything he could about this robbery that had altered Penny and Missy's lives and figure out what he could do to help them survive this nightmare.

Penny made scrambled eggs and toast for their breakfast and they ate it as the sun peeked over the horizon. She watched it from her window at their small kitchen table, not daring to step outside. Missy had dozed for a while after Caleb left but Penny hadn't been able to give up her guard enough to fall asleep. Last night had been a close call, and proof enough to her that they had indeed been found.

They were no longer safe here.

That knowledge scared her half to death. How had they been found? She thought she'd been so careful but she wasn't exactly an expert at hiding out. Somehow, somewhere, she must have given something away without even realizing it.

She had to do better for her daughter's sake.

She pushed the curtain aside. The police cruiser still sat at the curb in front of her house, alerting any would-be intruders, and her neighbors, that they were watching the house. She was thankful to Caleb for that but she couldn't depend on him providing that kind of security for them long-term.

She had to start thinking about themselves and how they were going to get out of town without being followed or killed.

She set up Missy with her coloring and a kids' movie, then picked up her prepaid cell phone and opened the internet search engine. She typed in what she needed and quickly scrolled through the site until she found the bus schedules. She didn't even care which direction they would go or where they would end up, but she was leaving Jessup on the next bus out of town.

She chose one, then went into the bedroom and packed her few belongings. She did the same with Missy's. As she was packing Missy's stuffed monkey and favorite blanket into her backpack, she spotted movement in the doorway. She gasped and looked up. Missy was standing there watching her, a picture in her hand.

Missy glanced at the backpack and cried out, shaking her head. While she still didn't say anything, Penny knew what she was thinking. She was tired of running. Penny was too, but what other choice did they have?

Penny pulled her into her arms. "I'm sorry, baby, but we have to go. We can't stay here anymore. It's not safe."

Missy groaned and pushed the picture she'd drawn into Penny's hand. She looked down at it. It was another image of red everywhere—a man lying dead on the floor and a man with a gun standing over him.

She dropped the picture as her heart broke. Her baby had seen so much violence in such a short amount of time. Of course, she would be traumatized. But Penny had to think about her safety before she could focus on dealing with her nightmares.

Somehow, some way, they were fleeing Jessup today.

# THREE

Caleb's alarm went off at 7:00 a.m. He showered and dressed, then headed downstairs. His body protested that it could use a few extra hours of sleep, but he was anxious to make sure Penny and Missy had made it through the rest of the night okay.

Of course, he knew he would have gotten a phone call if something had happened, but he still wanted to see for himself that they were safe.

It had been a long night but it wasn't the first time he'd functioned on only a few hours of sleep.

He hurried into the kitchen and saw his cousin Luke and his family finishing up breakfast. He shared the large ranch house at Harmon Ranch with Luke, his wife, Abby, and their two kids, Kenzie and Dustin.

Caleb and his cousins—Luke, Brett and Tucker—had each inherited a fourth of their grandfather's ranch when the old man passed away eight months ago. Luke had chosen to live here with his family while Brett had kept his part of the ranch but chosen to stay in Dallas to run his security firm. He and his wife, Jaycee, visited often. Meanwhile, Tucker had yet to show up to Harmon Ranch to claim his share. He'd promised to come and take care of the paperwork multiple times but always ended up canceling.

Caleb, of course, understood. None of them had good memories of growing up at Harmon Ranch or of their grandfather, Chet Harmon.

Caleb, unlike the rest of them, had lived at Harmon Ranch for years—ever since his mother had dropped him off when he was twelve to spend the summer with his grandfather. Only, she'd never returned to get him. He'd spent his remaining years being raised by his grandfather who, by that time, had become bitter and resentful with grief over the deaths of his four children. He'd had nothing left emotionally to give to his grandchildren…even the one living in his house.

"Good morning, Caleb," Abby said, smiling. "I made pancakes. Help yourself."

He poured himself a mug of coffee. "Thanks, but I'm not hungry. I'll grab something later at the station."

She glanced at the clock. "Is it that late? We've got to get going." She stood and hurried the kids. "Go grab your backpacks. We're leaving for school in five minutes." She leaned over and kissed Luke. "I've got to be going too or I'll be late for work."

"Have a good day," Luke called as his family hurried out the door.

Caleb slid into one of the empty chairs at the table. He'd been hoping for a few minutes with his cousin to talk over the issue of Penny Jackson. Luke had been an FBI agent for many years before settling down on the ranch. He often assisted Caleb and his investigators on cases and Caleb depended on his expertise. He should have some useful perspective to offer on Penny and Missy's case. "I need your advice. I met a woman yesterday."

Luke's mouth curved into an amused smile. "Really? Tell me about her."

He grimaced. Of course, his cousin would go directly to assuming it was a romantic involvement. Ever since reuniting with his high school girlfriend and gaining a family overnight, Luke and Abby both assumed everyone should find love. They liked to gently urge him to settle down with someone and be as blissful as they were. Although he was happy for them, relationships like that didn't happen for everyone. "It's not like that. She's in trouble. She's on the run with her six-year-old daughter."

Luke sat up straight. "What's going on?"

He and Luke had become like brothers over the past year since Luke had returned to Jessup, and Caleb was depending on his cousin's experience and insight to help him figure out how to best help Penny and Missy out of the mess they were in.

"There's a BOLO on her from the FBI. She's wanted as a material witness in a bank robbery that happened in Lexington, Kentucky, four months ago. The little girl can apparently ID the bank robbers. It's put their lives in danger so she took her daughter and ran. I've tried looking into the case but haven't been able to find out many details besides what was in the news about it. I was hoping—"

"You were hoping I could use my FBI connections to find out more?"

Caleb shrugged. Luke had recently retired from the FBI, but he still knew people in the Bureau.

He sighed and rubbed his face. "Let me make some calls. I'll see what I can find out."

Caleb tapped the table. "Thanks, cuz. I appreciate it. But, please, be discreet. I'd rather not have the FBI descending on Jessup looking for them. At least, not until I'm up to speed on what kind of danger they're really in."

"You know I will."

Someone was after them. That much he knew for certain. He'd witnessed it with his own eyes. He stood. "I'm heading over there now to talk to Penny."

Luke stood too and gave him a look. "Just answer one question for me. Why would you ignore a BOLO for a woman you hardly know?"

"What do you mean?"

"I mean, it's an FBI BOLO. You have an obligation to respond to it, but you didn't. Now, you're trying to hide her presence here from the FBI. That's not like you, Caleb. What's so special about her?"

He'd struggled with whether or not to contact the FBI immediately but had ultimately decided he had an obligation to the residents of Jessup too, to find out what was going on in his town. Now, after hearing Penny's story of being bullied by the feds, he knew he'd chosen correctly. "She and her daughter are in trouble. I want to make sure they're safe."

Luke frowned and Caleb could see his cousin felt that

the question hadn't been answered to his satisfaction. Caleb understood why Luke seemed uneasy. He could hardly even explain it to himself why he'd become so invested in what happened to these two.

"If you could see how protective she is of her daughter, you'd want to help her too. I mean, this lady has turned her entire world upside down just to make sure her daughter is safe. I admire that kind of love and devotion to your child. I just admire her, that's all."

Luke nodded. "I get it."

At first Caleb wasn't sure what he was referring to, but then he realized Luke was referencing Caleb's own relationship with his mother. "This has nothing to do with my mother," he insisted. "Can't I admire someone for their sacrifices without it having to do with my issues?"

Luke shrugged. "You can, but I sense it does."

Caleb's mother had unburdened herself of single motherhood after his father's death. She'd been too concerned about her career and her freedom to let the burden of raising him interfere with her plans.

He couldn't deny it was a far cry from the sacrifice Penny Jackson was making for her daughter.

"I admire her for giving up everything for her daughter, that's all."

Luke relented and stood. "I'll go contact some friends at the Bureau and see what I can find out about this case. And don't worry—I'll be discreet. They won't know she's here."

Caleb thanked him, then grabbed his hat and his gear and walked out to his pickup. He'd feel better having all the facts of the case before deciding how best to help Penny and Missy. The bad guys already knew she was in Jessup. It was only a matter of time before the feds knew it too.

Which meant they needed to figure out a plan for their safety fast.

Penny shoved what was left of her money into her pocket. It wasn't enough to get her very far without her identification, which she'd left in her purse inside her wrecked car, but her false name was burned anyway. She would have to think of something else—another way to get a new ID and replenish her cash. She hadn't started out with much to begin with. Only a few thousand dollars she'd managed to squirrel away for emergencies. Now, she was glad she had.

The emergency had hit her hard and fast.

She heard a car pull into her driveway, then voices filtered through the air. She hurried to the window.

Caleb was talking to the officer parked at the curb.

She grimaced. Why did he have to show up now?

She glanced at the time. There was a bus leaving Jessup heading toward Arizona in just over an hour and she planned for her and Missy to be on it.

She didn't have time for Caleb. Besides, he would surely try to stop them.

She ran and tossed the backpacks into the bedroom to hide them, then hurried to answer when he knocked on the front door.

He looked good and for a moment she was taken aback. He'd shaved and changed into a fresh uniform and his eyes sparkled as he smiled at her. In spite of herself, it caused her stomach to flip with excitement. She pushed away any thoughts of acting on her attraction to the handsome chief of police. She had a bus to catch, which meant Caleb Harmon would soon be out of her life for good.

He removed his cowboy hat as he stepped inside and closed the door behind him. "How are y'all doing this morning?"

His Texas drawl sent shivers through her.

*Stop that! What's wrong with you?* "We're doing okay," she told him. "We didn't get much sleep though."

"I imagine not." He walked over to Missy who was drawing on the floor. He knelt beside her. "What are you drawing, Missy?"

To Penny's surprise, Missy sat up and handed him the drawing she'd been working on. He studied it, then glanced at Penny. From where she was standing, she could see that it was yet another drawing of death and violence. A dead man on the floor and a man with a gun standing over him. Only today, Penny noticed the man with the gun was wearing a policeman's uniform like Caleb's.

Penny always assumed the men in the drawings were bad guys, but Missy didn't act frightened of Caleb. Was that her way instead of asking if Caleb was going to stop the bad guys chasing them?

Her heart squeezed at the thought that Missy trusted this man. She even inched closer to him as he spoke to her. It seemed like forever since her daughter had engaged with anyone but her.

Penny had never thought about getting married again after Devon was killed. She'd married him after finding out she was pregnant with Missy, but she'd known it was a mistake almost from day one. He'd been a drug user and a gambler and given away nearly every dollar they'd earned through his addictions.

After he'd died three years ago, she hadn't even thought about jumping into another romance. Yes, it would have been nice to have another person she could depend on during this nightmare, but Devon had proved to her that she couldn't depend on anyone but herself.

Caleb stood and walked to her as Missy turned back to drawing. He held out the picture and pointed to the man in uniform. "Is that supposed to be me?"

"I think so. She must believe you're going to help us take out the bad guys."

"I hope so. I want her, and you, to trust me. I don't like the idea of shooting anyone unless I have to but I appreciate the vote of confidence." He grinned. "I think she's warming up to me."

Unfortunately, she agreed with him, but they couldn't let sentimentality stand in their way.

He took her elbow and led her back into the kitchen. He lowered his voice so Missy couldn't overhear their conversation. She braced herself for what he was about to say, sensing he had news. "My cousin Luke used to be with the FBI. I asked him to see what he could find out about your case."

All of her defenses went up. "Why did you do that? Now they'll know where we are." It was worrying enough that her attackers had found her. Now, she'd have to dodge the FBI as well.

"Don't worry. He'll be discreet. I just want to know what we're dealing with so I'll know how to best keep you and Missy safe."

While she appreciated his intention, he had no idea what he was getting into. "You can't keep us safe, Caleb. I appreciate the guard at my house but how long can that go on? And how can we be sure that will keep those men away? They haven't hesitated to take out the person guarding me before. We need to disappear from the bad guys and the authorities. I'd hoped to do that here but obviously I messed up. I'll do better this time—because there's no other option. I have to keep my daughter safe."

"You can't do this on your own, Penny. You need to trust me. I'll do what I can to get you both out of this."

She saw his determination. He wanted to help and she truly did appreciate his willingness… Only he had no idea what he was getting involved in. It was much better for everyone if she didn't allow him to. She could see that he wasn't going to give up on his own but maybe he would once she was out of his jurisdiction and vanished.

"I've got my officers taking shifts on watching your house. They'll alert me if they see anything suspicious. I want you to call me too if you hear or see anything. I'm going to follow up with my cousin." His phone beeped and he glanced at the screen. "That's him now. He wants to meet me back at the station. I'll swing by later and let you know what he says. I can also pick up some takeout for supper if you'd like."

She nodded and gave him a smile. "That would be nice." It would be too, except that they weren't going to be here for supper. But she would say anything to get him out the door. She glanced at the clock again. Less than an hour until their bus left town.

She watched him leave and was saddened at the thought that she was deceiving him. He'd done everything he could to help them and here she was betraying his trust. Maybe someday she would get the chance to explain but, for now, she had to do what she thought was best for Missy.

She watched him through the window as he climbed into his vehicle and drove away. Now was their chance.

She pulled out her cell phone and called for a cab, using her backyard neighbor's address. She grabbed their backpacks and slipped them on, then pushed her cell phone into her pocket. She would ditch this one at the bus station and purchase another one when they reached Arizona.

Missy didn't protest when Penny carefully opened the back door and they slipped out. Penny did her best not to alert the officer watching the house. She hurried across the backyard and quickly helped Missy over the fence, then climbed it herself, thankful when she dropped into her neighbor's yard without anyone calling after her or seeming to notice her at all.

While she'd kept to herself and hadn't really bothered to get to know her neighbors, she'd paid close attention to their comings and goings, and she'd seen that they were gone during the day. That was good—it meant there was no one home to ask what she was doing. When they'd first arrived in town and she'd rented this house, she'd hoped at least one of her neighbors had a dog to alert her to any intruders in the area. Now, she was thankful none of them did so they could sneak out without being spotted.

They crouched in the bushes until she spotted the cab pull up at the curb, then they hurried to it.

"Here we are," she called to the cabdriver before he could get out and knock on the door. She opened the back door and they slid inside the cab. "We're going to the bus station," she reiterated, having already given their destination when she called for the cab.

The driver nodded and started the meter as he pulled away. Missy stared out the window, looking forlorn at having to run again. One day, her daughter would understand. For now, this was what she had to do.

She only hoped that one day Caleb could forgive her for not trusting him enough.

Caleb hurried back to the police station. Luke was already there in his office waiting for him. His cousin looked flushed.

"It's about time."

"What is it?" Caleb asked. "You found something?"

"I sure did." He opened his laptop and pulled up some images before giving a description of the robbery that matched Penny's—including Missy being the only one to see any of the robbers unmasked. "This group has been hitting banks throughout six states," Luke continued, "including one incident where two police officers were killed. The feds have been itching to find evidence to tie them to these robberies and bring them to justice. The girl's testimony was going to be the heart of their case."

Caleb folded his arms and scowled as the weight of the situation Penny and Missy were in hit him. He clicked on one of the men's photos and read through his charges and background. "So then they're all in jail?"

"They were. The case wasn't strong enough without Missy, so the federal prosecutor was forced to drop the charges against them—but they can refile once they locate her. The men were released early this morning."

Obviously, these men had influence even while they were incarcerated since the two men who had broken into Penny's home and then run her off the road couldn't have been any of them. Now, with known killers out on the loose, they would certainly be coming after Missy in order to preserve their freedom.

"Did the whole case really depend on a six-year-old's identification? Don't they have other evidence?"

"Everything they've gathered originated with Missy's identification. Without that, the case falls apart. It's a risk to put a child that young under oath but it's all they have at the moment." Luke stepped toward him. "She has to testify, Caleb. Each of these criminals are dangerous on their own, but she could take this entire operation down. And now that a federal agent has been killed, the men could face charges for that as well. There's no statute of limitations on murder. As long as the girl is alive, she could bring them a world of trouble at any time just by agreeing to testify. With that risk hanging over their heads, they'll never stop coming after her."

That was the same thought he'd had.

"You have to convince this woman that she needs to allow her daughter to take the witness stand. Right now, WITSEC is their best option to keep them safe. I have a friend I can call—Marissa. She's a US Marshal. I know her and trust her. It's their best chance of staying alive."

His jaw tensed. He agreed with Luke. This situation was much worse than he'd thought. The bad guys had already discovered them here in Jessup. It wouldn't be long before the entire gang came after them. This group could not allow Missy to live.

He had to convince Penny that witness protection was their best option. The government had the means and resources to keep them safe long-term. "I'll talk to her and try to make her see the light."

His phone rang and he checked the caller ID. Officer Dale Mason. Caleb had left him to guard Penny and Missy's house. Something must be wrong if he was calling.

He hit the button to answer the call. "Mason, what's happened?"

"I'm sorry, Chief. She's gone."

He glanced up at Luke. "What do you mean she's gone? Someone took her?"

"No, she bolted. I saw a cab pass by in my rearview mirror and I thought I saw her in the back. I went inside to check on them and the house was empty. I think she left on her own."

He sighed and the truth of Mason's words hit him.

Looking back on it now, he realized that she had given in to his offer of bringing by supper awfully fast. It hadn't been a sign of her starting to accept his help but rather of her saying whatever she thought would get him out the door the fastest…so she could make her escape.

Of course she was planning to leave town without telling him.

He rubbed his neck. "Thanks for letting me know. Head back to the station and we'll come up with a plan." He ended the call. "She bolted."

Luke ran a hand through his hair. "We've got to find her before these guys do."

He tried to think logically. "She doesn't have a car so, if she's leaving town, she would have to do so some other way." There weren't a lot of public transportation options available in a small town like Jessup. "She has to be headed to the bus station."

Luke followed him outside to his truck and they climbed inside. He was glad to have his cousin backing him up but he also called for a team to meet them at the station in case the men who'd come after her previously came looking for her there as well.

Frustration bit through him. Why hadn't she remained at the house where she'd been safe? Why hadn't she trusted him?

He knew the truth. She didn't trust anyone and she would do anything to protect her daughter, even something foolish like fleeing town. He had no idea how he was going to convince her not to run, but he had to do so. He had to convince her that witness protection was their only option.

It may be the only way to keep both her and Missy alive.

Penny purchased two tickets to Phoenix, then sat and waited for the bus to begin loading. She pulled out her cell phone. Now was the time to dispose of it so no one could use it to track them. She walked over to the trash can, ready to toss it in, but startled when the phone rang.

She glanced at the screen. Caleb. Did he know yet that she was gone? If she didn't answer, he might discover it sooner than she'd hoped.

Of course, if she answered it, that might give him the answer too.

She couldn't be sure which option was safest, so she hit the answer key, simply because he'd been nice to her and he deserved an explanation.

"Hello."

"Penny, what are you doing?"

So he knew already. "This for the best, Caleb. Thank you for all you've done for us but we're better off just disappearing."

"That's not true. I've seen the files. I know the kind of people you're messing with. They will find you. You have to let us help you."

She heard the plea in his voice and she wanted to give in. He was the only person who'd tried to help them. But she couldn't drag him any further into her problem. "I can't. I'm sorry, Caleb." She ended the call, then tossed the phone into the trash can.

She turned to see him standing behind her, a disappointed look on his face. He slid his cell phone back into his pocket.

"You won't change my mind," she insisted. "We're getting on that bus."

"Listen, Penny, I can't make you do anything but running isn't the answer. These men are brutal and they won't stop coming after you."

"That's why we have to leave."

"They found you here. They'll find you wherever you go. They've got all the connections and resources that you don't."

She ran a hand through her hair, frustrated because she recognized that everything he said was the truth. But what other option did she have? "What am I supposed to do? I have to protect her."

He closed the gap between them. "Let me help you. My cousin Luke has a friend at the marshal service. She's willing to help you. She'll take you both into protective custody and keep you safe."

She shook her head. "That'll mean testifying, which will just make those men more determined to come after Missy, and I can't risk it. They already found us in FBI protection. How do I know we'll be safe with the Marshals?"

"My cousin knows this marshal. He trusts her and I trust his judgment." He stared at her and sighed. "They're already coming after Missy. At least, this way, you'll have someone else watching your backs."

She leaned against him as the weight of the world spun her. She wanted to do the right thing by Missy but was she making the right choice by running? What if Caleb was right that witness protection was a better option? So far, running and hiding hadn't been that successful. These men had found her hundreds of miles away in a town where she had no connections. She still didn't understand what she'd done wrong that had tipped them off to her whereabouts.

"Caleb!"

They both turned to see a man heading their way.

"We spotted the truck from the BOLO driving around the lot."

She felt him tense. "They're here."

He grabbed her arm and pulled her to the bench where Missy was sitting. He scooped her daughter up into his arms and pushed them both against a back wall while the man who'd called to him—obviously his cousin—along with several officers, drew their weapons and stood ready.

Caleb drew his gun too but remained beside them. His breathing kicked up a notch but he stood planted in place, a solid shield to protect them. She was in awe of his strength and determination, especially given how hard she was trying to push him away.

His team remained visible through the glass entrance doors.

She could see past them and spotted the truck that had run her off the road. It slowly drove by the entrance. Her pulse pounded and she pulled Missy against her. It was the two men who'd attacked her the previous night. They'd found her here. If Caleb hadn't come, they would probably have dragged her and Missy from the bus.

They slow-crawled past the entrance, then sped off, obviously seeing the armed protection detail standing just inside.

"Go after them," Caleb instructed, and a group of four officers hurried away.

Luke turned to them. "That was close."

Caleb breathed a sigh of relief and nodded. "Agreed." He holstered his weapon, then turned to Penny. "Luke, this is Penny. Penny, this is my cousin Luke. You can trust him."

She was shaking so hard on the inside that she thought she might fall apart. Hot tears pressed against the backs of her eyes but she refused to let them drop. She'd nearly gotten herself and her daughter killed with her stubborn determination to do this her own way. She'd made the wrong decision and placed Missy's life in danger.

"You know this marshal?" she asked Luke.

He nodded, then gave her a kind smile. "I do. She'll take good care of you both. I promise."

She turned to Caleb and nodded. "Okay, I'll do it." She fell into his embrace and he wrapped his arms around her without question.

"Good. You don't have to do this alone anymore, Penny. I'll be right there with you and Missy while Luke arranges for you to meet with the marshal. I'll make sure you're safe until she takes you into protective custody."

She was grateful for his help after the way she'd betrayed him. They needed him. She needed him.

And suddenly she realized she wasn't alone in this any longer.

# FOUR

Caleb loaded Penny and Missy into his truck. He left several of his officers behind to secure the scene while Luke followed Caleb to make certain they weren't ambushed on the way back to the police station.

He watched the rearview mirrors too on the way back, to ensure they weren't followed. He would keep Penny and Missy at the police station while Luke made the arrangements to hand them off to the US Marshals for safekeeping.

He parked behind the building, then got out and walked around to the passenger's side where he scooped Missy up into his arms. She laid her head on his shoulder while he walked, with Penny ahead of him, through the back door.

Several people looked up as they entered the building. His team knew what was happening but he felt the need to explain. "Everyone be on alert," he told them. "This is Penny and her daughter, Missy. It's our job to keep them safe until they can enter witness protection."

Jana Stewart, one of his patrol officers, spoke up.

"Don't worry. We'll lock down the office, Chief. No one will get in."

He was grateful for his team. Penny and Missy needed them now.

Caleb led Penny through the police station and into his private office. "There's a couch in here where you two can get some rest. Luke is contacting his friend at the Marshals' office so it shouldn't be long."

Missy climbed from his arms and onto the couch and stretched out. It was obvious she was worn out and who could blame her? He doubted either her or Penny had gotten a good night's rest since the bank robbery incident.

Penny unzipped Missy's backpack and pulled out a pink blanket. She draped it over her, then tucked the stuffed monkey in with her. "She always sleeps better with Monkey."

"You should get some rest too. I promise you, you're safe here. No one is getting into this office. There's a TV and a private bathroom you can use."

"I don't want to put you out of your own office," she insisted.

He waved away her concerns. "I can work out of the conference room just down the hall. It's not a problem."

She turned to him and looked up into his eyes. Caleb felt his breath catch. She was so beautiful, but it was the determination in her eyes that drew her to him. She was so determined to keep her daughter safe. He admired that and wanted to help her.

"Well, we appreciate it regardless." She sat on the couch and laid her head on the cushion. Her body seemed to relax right away.

He turned off the lights and closed the door behind him. They would be safe here for now.

He walked down the corridor to the conference room. Luke was already there on the phone. He hung up when Caleb entered.

"Did you reach out to your friend?"

"I did. She's going to get back to me as soon as she has something set up. Until then, we keep them under guard here."

Caleb nodded. "Agreed." He walked into the next room and spoke to his technicians. "Have there been any hits on the pickup we saw at the bus station?"

"According to the plates, the truck was stolen from a factory three towns over. We've set up roadblocks in and out of town but, so far, we haven't located it, and no calls have come in from anyone spotting it."

"What about prints from the house? Did we have any hits?"

"We didn't get any prints from the house, Chief. Looks like the men wore gloves. We got some shoe prints, but they didn't tell us much aside from shoe size, and we couldn't find any hairs or fibers that didn't belong to the occupants."

He rubbed his face. He'd been hoping for a lead to a suspect they could arrest to end the threat against them once and for all.

But the truth was that even an arrest of the men in question wouldn't stop it. He suspected these assailants were only hired hands in town to do a job. If they were arrested, more would come to take their place. Maybe even the same men Missy had initially identified—the ones who had been let out of jail that morning.

"Okay, let's keep an eye on the town borders and make sure these men don't get away. I also want to pull the mug shots of the bank robbers. They were released today. We don't want them sneaking into town."

Caleb kept up with the roadblocks and video surveillance all afternoon but, unfortunately, no sign of the men who'd targeted Penny and Missy were found. They'd gone underground quickly.

Finally, his cousin hurried into the room.

"It's about time," Caleb told him. "What's taking so long?"

"Bureaucratic red tape. Marissa is on board but she has to have the official paperwork in place before she can take Penny and Missy into protective custody."

"What does that entail?"

Luke hesitated. "The US Attorney has to approve it. Penny will have to sign an agreement stating Missy will testify against the bank robbers."

He nodded. "I think I can convince her to make that choice."

"I had them e-mail the form to me." He handed the paper over. "She'll need to sign it, then Marissa can make all the arrangements."

He nodded. "She's resting in my office. I'll take this to her."

He knocked on his office door, then opened it. The room was still dark but he could see that Penny's eyes were open. When he stepped in, she stood and faced him. Missy was still sleeping with her head on the armrest.

"Is it time?" Anxiousness shone in her voice.

"Not yet. The US Attorney has to approve witness protection before the marshal can make the arrangements." He held up the paper Luke had given him. "We printed out a form for you to sign saying that you'll allow Missy to testify."

Her shoulders slumped and he could see she was hesitant.

"I know you still have some doubts, but this is the best thing for both of you. The marshals can keep you and Missy safe. My cousin knows this marshal personally. He trusts her and I trust him."

She nodded. "I know I have to do this. If they found us here, they can find us anywhere. I'll sign it."

He grabbed a pen from his desk and watched as she signed the agreement. He glanced over at Missy who was still sleeping soundly. He was glad that she was getting some—probably much-needed—rest and glad as well that with Penny signing this form, Missy would now have access to something else that she badly needed. "Trials take a long time and getting Missy to open up will be important for the feds. They'll make sure she gets the psychological help she needs to deal with everything she's been through."

She nodded and he noticed tears of relief in her eyes.

She handed the paper back to him. "How long will we have to wait after they receive this before the marshal can move us somewhere safe?"

"I'm not sure, but I think the best thing is for you both to remain here until then. Those men are still out there. We haven't located them yet. Plus, I learned earlier that they had to release the bank robbers this morning, so we're on the lookout for them as well. The sooner we can get you both out of town and into protective custody with the Marshals, the better."

She nodded. "We'll stay wherever you think is best for as long as it takes."

Missy stirred on the couch and Penny rushed to her side.

"I'm going to have someone bring some food in for you two. I'd prefer you stay in here for now. I have a private bathroom you can use, plus there's a TV and an iPad if she likes to watch videos."

She nodded and pulled Missy to her. "We're fine with that. Missy has her crayons."

He hurried out and passed the signed agreement on to his cousin, who took it from him with a relieved smile. "I'll e-mail this to Marissa right now," Luke promised.

"Find out if she can give you an ETA on when she can meet to take them. I'm worried that keeping them here in town for much longer is dangerous."

"I'm on it."

Luke hurried into the conference room and pulled out his laptop. Caleb turned to one of his officers. "Can you order in some food for Penny and Missy? They're going to be here for a while longer."

"Sure thing, Chief."

He was getting frustrated by the fact that they couldn't find the men. Everyone had been alerted right away and had been on the lookout for them since the bus station. Before that, even—since they'd run Penny and Missy off the road. Yet, the attackers had still managed to disappear. He kept his officers on high alert all afternoon and well into the night. He also forwarded images of the bank robbers to all his patrol officers. If any of these men arrived in town, he wanted to know about it.

Luke stayed on the phone, pressing for information about a placement for Penny and Missy. However they were at the mercy of the US Attorney's office and they were slow in getting back with them. Luke's marshal friend couldn't act until given the okay.

So they waited.

A driver delivered food and Caleb carried it into the office. Missy was jumping around and playing. He was glad to see that.

"She has so much energy," Penny explained. "I hope she's not being too loud."

Caleb smiled. "Not at all. She's not hurting anything."

Penny dumped some French fries and chicken nuggets from the food bag onto a plate, then called Missy over to eat. The little girl dug into her food, but Penny only picked at hers.

"Are you scared?" Caleb asked her. He knew she was but he wanted to say something that would get her talking.

She nodded. "I wish I'd never gone to that bank. I wish none of this had ever happened."

She had been through a lot so he could understand her frustrations. She only wanted to keep her daughter safe but they'd been targeted and hunted—not to mention let down by the people who were supposed to protect them.

"I can't promise you that everything will be completely better once you're in witness protection, but at least you'll be safe and you can get Missy the help she needs."

She brushed away a stray tear and nodded. "We owe you, Caleb. I know that if you hadn't come after us, those men would have caught us today."

"You're here, and that's all that matters now. There's no point in worrying about the past."

"I thought I could keep her safe but I was fooling myself. Hiding was so hard. I still don't even know how they found us."

"You did your best."

"It wasn't enough."

"It *was* enough. It got you this far, Penny. Don't put yourself down for trying to protect your child. It's more than a lot of people would do."

She shook her head. "What mother wouldn't do whatever it took to keep her child safe?"

He bit his tongue. She didn't seem aware that there were mothers out there that wouldn't do half of what she'd done to protect their kids. He didn't even want her to realize that people like that existed.

His office door opened and Luke darted in. "I just spoke to my friend, Marissa. She got the all clear from the US Attorney's office to proceed. She's making the arrangements for your safe house. She said we could meet her in three hours to make the handoff."

Caleb stood. "Good, good. Where are we meeting her?"

"I gave her directions to a diner I know about an hour and a half away."

He was glad Luke hadn't invited her to come to Jessup. He preferred making a drive. It gave him plenty of time to make sure they weren't being followed.

He turned back to Penny and saw apprehension on her face. She twisted her hands.

"Everything is going to be okay now," he assured her.

"I hope you're right." She cleaned up the trash from their food, then gathered their things together.

He prayed he was right too. He hated to see someone trying so hard to do the right thing and getting nothing but trouble in return.

Caleb was tense as they drove to the meet-up. Penny could see his jaw tighten and his knuckles whiten from his grip on the steering wheel as he constantly checked his mirrors to make certain they weren't being followed by anyone other than Luke, who was following behind them as an added precaution.

She was thankful for Caleb's attention to their safety. She and Missy were depending on him and, so far, he was rising to the challenge.

He turned off a narrow highway and into the parking lot of a diner. The restaurant's neon sign glowed in the night sky. The parking lot was nearly empty at this time of night. She unbuckled Missy and they got out and walked inside. A waitress greeted them and showed them to a table. She ordered Missy a stack of pancakes with strawberry syrup. She chose only dry toast for herself, not sure she'd be able to stomach anything more, while Caleb ordered coffee.

Luke entered the diner and slid into a booth on the opposite side of the room a few minutes before their food arrived. He and Caleb exchanged glances, seemingly speaking a secret language between them. But they both seemed calm, which she supposed meant that everything was good and they hadn't been followed.

Penny's hands shook as she cut up Missy's pancakes. When she was finished and Missy dug in, Caleb reached across the table and held Penny's hand.

"Everything is going to be all right," he assured her.

She needed his confidence. Despite placing her trust in this man, she was still reeling from nearly being abducted and killed. The latest incident only proved to her that she didn't have the skills necessary to keep her daughter safe by herself.

She was thankful for Caleb's intervention and for the Marshals ensuring their protection, yet she was still scared. Both their lives were still in danger.

She glanced around. They were supposed to be meeting the marshal but they'd been there for twenty minutes and she still hadn't arrived. "Where is she?"

"Marshal Dryer said she would be here at ten. It's not quite ten yet."

They'd arrived early so Caleb could scope out the diner in advance. He'd said that he didn't want any surprises. Penny had agreed with the idea, wanting this handoff to go as smoothly as possible. She tried not to fret, but their safety was in the hands of these people she'd only just met.

She spotted Caleb tense and turned to see a car pull into the parking lot. A woman dressed in slacks and a blazer—that only partially hid the gun holstered at her side—walked into the diner. Her whole demeanor screamed federal agent, even to Penny's untrained eyes.

Caleb moved across the table, sliding in beside Penny who scooted Missy down the seat as the woman stopped to greet Luke, then the two of them approached the booth.

She slid into the seat he'd just vacated, then reached to shake his hand. "Caleb? It's nice to meet you. Thank you for the call." She looked at Missy, then Penny. "My name is Marshal Marissa Dryer. I'll be taking point on your case, Ms. Jackson. I'm glad you finally decided to do the smart thing and come in out of the cold."

Penny still wasn't sure this was a good idea, but she'd accepted it. "What choice do I have? I thought I could end this nightmare if I made it clear my daughter wouldn't testify, yet those men still keep coming after us. I have to do what I can to protect Missy from them."

"I assure you—I'll do everything I can to keep you both safe."

Marshal Dryer gave off an air of confidence that Penny liked. She glanced at Luke then Caleb, who gave her a nod to indicate it was going to be okay. He'd made it clear he thought this was the best course for them. The Marshals had the resources to keep them protected and safe, much more than he did.

Marshal Dryer stood. "Good. Ready to go then?"

Penny used the napkin to wipe syrup from Missy's mouth and hands as Caleb slid from the booth. Penny and Missy stood too and waited while Caleb left money on the table for their food.

She clasped Missy's hand and followed Marshal

Dryer to the door. Caleb kept his hand on her back as they walked and his gentle touch helped nudge her forward. The uncertainty of what they were facing frightened her but this was what needed to be done, so she marched toward it, hoping against hope that she was making the right choice for their future.

Yet, the worst part at that moment was saying goodbye to Caleb. He was the first person in a long time who she'd come to trust. She glanced up at him and he looked like he wanted to say something. She felt the same pull that seemed to mirror in his eyes. How could she be so attached to a man she'd just met?

Caleb turned to the marshal. "Can we have a minute to say goodbye?"

Marshal Dryer nodded. "I'll be in the car."

"I'll walk you out," Luke stated. "Meet you outside," he told Caleb.

They exited the diner and Caleb turned back to Penny. There was so much she wanted to say to him but she was suddenly at a loss for words. They'd only known one another for a short time, yet he'd become so important to her. "Missy and I owe you much more than thanks, Caleb. I don't even know how to say thank you. It doesn't seem enough."

"Just keep Missy safe. That'll be enough thanks for me. I have a good feeling about Marshal Dryer."

She glanced at the marshal sitting and waiting in her vehicle. She'd had a kind smile along with that reassuring air of confidence. "Yes, I think she does seem to care. Anyway, I guess it is the best plan to keep Missy safe. That's what really matters."

He reached for her hands and held them. "I know you won't be able to contact me once you enter the program but I want you to know that I admire you, Penny, and everything you're doing for your daughter. Stay safe and keep her close to you."

She nearly teared up. She wasn't sure she deserved his admiration after how she'd nearly gotten them captured and killed, but his words meant a lot to her. "I will."

He walked them outside, stopping at his own pickup to grab their few belongings.

They were nearly at the marshal's car when Missy pulled on her shirt. Penny looked down at the girl, then back at Caleb. "I should take her to the bathroom before we get on the road."

He leaned into the car to let the marshal know the change in plans as Missy urged Penny back toward the diner. Caleb was right behind them when suddenly an explosion sent them reeling.

Penny hit the ground hard, the asphalt stinging her hands and legs. Through the smoke, she spotted Missy whimpering a few inches away. When she was able, she crawled closer. Tears rolled down her daughter's face and blood from a cut was smeared across her cheek. Penny quickly checked her over. Physically, the injuries were superficial.

Penny pulled her into an embrace as she glanced back at the marshal's car which was now a blaze of fire.

Someone rushed past her, startling her because she hadn't heard the footsteps. She realized her ears were still ringing from the blast and she had no idea what was happening around her.

She saw Luke kneel and only then realized that Caleb was still on the ground. She screamed his name and Luke looked at her.

"He's alive," he said, although his words were obscured by the ringing in her ears.

Moments later, Caleb flinched, then stumbled to his feet with his cousin's help.

Penny grabbed up her daughter, ran to him and let him lean on her too for support. He wrapped one arm around them as he stared back at the car. Soot covered his face and his expression was grim.

She knew he must be thinking about Marshal Dryer who'd been inside that car when it exploded. There was no way she could have survived. Penny's ears were still ringing but she thought she heard Luke say the word *bomb*.

She shuddered. As sad as she felt for the deceased marshal—and for Caleb's cousin, who had been the marshal's friend—she admittedly felt a little guilty relief that she and Missy hadn't been casualties too. After all, they'd nearly been inside that car when it went off.

"Let's go. Back into my truck," Caleb said, pushing them toward it.

Penny didn't hesitate. She ran to the pickup. It wasn't safe here anymore. The bomb that had exploded the marshal's car might have been on a timer or it might have been set by someone lurking in the darkness. Whichever it was, they needed to get away before anyone showed up to finish the job of taking her and Missy out.

She climbed into the pickup with Missy and Caleb slid behind the wheel. He shook his head to clear it and she could see he was still feeling the effects of the explosion. He didn't let it stop him from peeling out.

As they sped away, she spotted Luke standing in the dark parking lot and the marshal's burning car lighting up the night sky.

# FIVE

Penny's heart hammered and she struggled for each breath as they fled the scene of the explosion.

She held tight to Missy, so much so that the girl squirmed to be released. She reluctantly did so before digging through her bag to find something to wipe away the blood and dirt from Missy's face. As she pulled things from the backpack, Missy grabbed hold of her stuffed monkey and clung to it. Penny didn't object, understanding that her daughter needed the comfort of her favorite toy. She found a Band-Aid and placed it over the cut on Missy's cheek.

Her own hands were scraped from hitting the pavement and she did her best to clean them with what she had in her bag. Her jeans were ripped at the knee but that wasn't a big deal. Their injuries were surprisingly minor considering how close they'd come to losing their lives again. If they hadn't turned to go to the bathroom, they would have been inside that car with Marshal Dryer when the bomb exploded.

She shuddered again, thinking about Marshal Dryer.

She'd seemed like a nice person and now she was dead because she'd tried to help them.

"Someone must have followed her to the meeting."

Penny wasn't sure if Caleb was speaking to her or just thinking aloud but she did know he'd been careful to make certain no one had followed them. He and his cousin had made sure of that.

"But how would they have known we were meeting her?" she asked Caleb, keeping her voice low as Missy nodded off to sleep against her.

His jaw clenched as he shook his head. "I've been asking myself that question too. I don't have the answers."

"What do we do now?"

He sighed and rubbed a hand over his jaw as he mulled over their situation. "My grandfather has an old fishing cabin on the outskirts of Jessup. It's isolated and few people even know it exists. You and Missy should be safe there until we figure this out."

She was glad he had another plan. Once again, he'd come through for them. They might be dead now if not for him.

She leaned her head against the seat and tried to let the darkness filling the cabin of Caleb's pickup soothe her as they headed back toward Jessup and the remote cabin. She didn't know where she was. She only hoped her assailants didn't know either.

Missy kept whimpering in her sleep as Caleb drove. He took the long way, hoping to disappear into the darkness of night. They needed to vanish and fast. If the men who were after Penny and Missy had the power to take out a US Marshal, then they were in even more trouble than he'd first believed.

His mind was spinning with all the terrible possibilities. Whoever had placed that bomb in the marshal's car had known Penny and Missy would be there but, to his knowledge, only a few people knew that they were even meeting with Marshal Dryer. The bad guys had to have known Dryer was coming to meet with her. Someone had alerted the criminals to their plan. There was a leak and it could be anywhere—the FBI, US Marshals or even the US Attorney's office.

It angered him to think that someone would leak the location of an innocent little girl to a group of monsters trying to kill her.

He was sixty miles out of town before he turned off a back road and onto a dirt one. His grandfather's fishing cabin was still half a mile off the road and as secluded as one could get. He'd come up here a lot with his dad when he was little. He and his cousins had fished and hunted here just about as far back as he could remember. But that had been years ago, back before his father and uncles had died. Once his grandfather had lost his sons, he'd also lost his will to bring his grandchild to the cabin. It had been abandoned for a decade until Caleb had rediscovered it a few years back and restored it to a livable condition. Since then, he'd visited often. It was a great place to get away and, over the years, Caleb had spent countless days hiding out from life here—fishing, hunting and spending alone time getting his heart right with the Lord. It was his own personal quiet place that no one knew about. Even his cousins, who had been there so many times in the past, might struggle to re-member where the old cabin could be found. He hadn't brought anyone there in years.

Now, it was going to serve as Penny and Missy's safe place.

His headlights rolled over the small cabin and he parked close to the door and cut the engine. He glanced over to see Missy wrapped in her mother's arms and Penny asleep against the headrest. She looked so peace-ful that he hated to disturb her, but the sooner they got inside, the safer they would be.

He reached out and touched her shoulder. She jerked awake instantly. "We're here," he told her.

She nodded, sat up and looked around. "It's so dark."

"Where we are there aren't any streetlights or out-side illumination. There is a motion sensor light out-side the door but it needs to be changed and I haven't gotten around to it. I'll make sure that's done. It'll alert us if someone approaches the cabin. In the meantime though, I wouldn't worry. Probably, the only movement you'll find are deer and other wildlife."

He got out and carried a still sleeping Missy into the cabin. Penny pushed open the door, stepped inside and glanced around. He wondered what she thought of it—if she saw it as shabby. The place was dusty, that was for sure. It had been over a year since he'd even been here, and the lack of recent cleaning showed. Still, the place appeared to be intact. He brought Missy into the bedroom and put her down, then stepped back into the main room. Penny was still surveying the small living area and the open kitchen.

"It needs a good cleaning but it should all be perfectly functional. And the best part is no one knows about this place and there are no neighbors for miles. You two should be safe here."

She opened a cupboard and he spotted several cans of soup but not much more. They would need supplies and it was too late at night to go. "I can bring some groceries tomorrow."

She turned to him and smiled. "It's fine. We'll make do. Don't worry about us."

"There's not exactly a grocery store nearby."

"It's okay, Caleb. We've gotten used to living light. None of us were expecting this."

She walked to the table and fell into a chair, then rubbed her hands over her face. "I can't believe this is happening. How do you think they found us?" Even though Missy was sleeping, Penny lowered her voice when talking about their perilous situation.

He shook his head. "I wish I knew. They could have been tipped off by a mole in the FBI or Marshals' offices maybe. They knew she was meeting us. They must have followed her to the rendezvous or tapped her phone and got the details that way. I'm not sure yet exactly who the source could have been, but we need to find out."

She rubbed her hands over her arms and shuddered. It was natural for her to be shaken. It had been an incredibly close call.

He pulled out a chair opposite her and sat down. "This is a setback for sure, but I promise you—we will figure this out. Luke stayed behind at the diner and will be in touch with the Marshals and FBI. We'll probably know more by the morning. I'll meet-up with him then and find out what they know."

She nodded but he could see it was going to take time for her to settle down. Maybe once she realized they were safe here, she could finally relax.

"Why don't you go lie down and try to rest. I'll stand guard—for tonight, anyway. I want to be back at my office first thing tomorrow morning to link up with Luke and get an update." He pulled out a cell phone and placed it on the table. "I turned off location services so no one can track this phone. It's a prepaid number. No one has the number except for me. It was still in my truck from an undercover sting my office participated in a few months back. I'll leave it with you when I go into town in the morning. I've programmed my number into it but, after tonight, the feds will likely be monitoring my cell phone calls. Only use it in case of an emergency. I'll stop tomorrow and get another burner phone so we can keep in touch without being detected."

She picked up the cell phone and slipped it into her pocket. "I understand."

"I'll stay the night on the couch, then head back tomorrow evening after work."

"Won't the feds be following you?"

He nodded. "I'm sure they will but I know how to lose a tail. I won't let them follow me here." He could see she was still worried and she had every right to be. He reached across the table and took her hand, trying to reassure her. "Penny, we will figure this out together."

She squeezed his hand, then stood. "I think I will go

lie down with Missy. She'll be awake and needing my attention soon enough."

"If you're still sleeping when I leave, I'll lock up."

"Thank you for all your help, Caleb."

He watched her disappear into the bedroom and shut the door.

He blew out a breath, then reached for his cell phone to let Luke know that they were safe and that he would be in touch in the morning. Then, he scrounged for a screwdriver to fix the outside light.

Penny and Missy were still sleeping when Caleb left the cabin at the break of dawn. He hated leaving without letting Penny know but he also didn't want to disturb their sleep. They both needed it after the last few nights they'd endured.

He headed back into Jessup and arrived at the police station before the day shift reported for duty. He checked in with the dispatcher and learned it had been a quiet night—only one drunk and disorderly call. His officers knew their jobs and they had procedures in place. They didn't need Caleb micromanaging everything they did and he was glad of that.

He showered and changed into a fresh uniform in his private bathroom. His cousin was waiting for him when he was done.

"How are they?" Luke asked.

"They're safe for now." He trusted Luke more than just about anyone but he still decided to keep their location from him. "What happened with the Marshals?"

"They're in a frenzy over Marissa's death." Caleb

noticed the grim look on Luke's face and could see the death had shaken Luke as well.

"I'm sorry about your friend."

"Thank you. She was a good person. She didn't deserve to die that way."

"Do they know anything more about the explosion?"

He nodded. "They've been working all night. It was a homemade bomb. All the ingredients are cheap and easily obtained so it won't be easy to trace them back to a person. It was on a timer and video surveillance shows it was placed on Marissa's car while she was in the diner. If Penny hadn't stopped to take the little girl to the bathroom, they would have both been inside the car with Marissa."

So a restroom stop had actually saved their lives. Unbelievable. "You said video captured someone setting the bomb. Do we have an identification?"

"No. His face wasn't visible. However, based on an approximate body shape and size, the FBI has already determined it wasn't any of the men arrested as part of the bank robbery."

Caleb rubbed his face. "That's not surprising. The men who attacked Penny and Missy in their house and then on the road couldn't have been any of them since they were still in jail when the attacks first occurred. They had to have been working for the group. This guy too, assuming it wasn't one of the men who attacked her here in Jessup."

Luke nodded. "The FBI is looking into known associates of the bank robbers."

"And do you think they will share any information they find with us?"

He shook his head. "Doubtful. The lead agent on the case is a woman named Rose Sinclair. I knew her during my time with the Bureau but we weren't exactly friends. We worked a case together and clashed professionally. I was the agent in charge. At one point, we were brainstorming operational options as a group and I chose someone else's idea over hers. She thought her idea was better than the one I landed on. She wasn't happy with me then and, I suspect, she won't be in a sharing mood now."

Although Caleb was glad to have his cousin's Bureau connections most of the time, he hated the bureaucracy and competitiveness that accompanied it. No wonder Luke had taken early retirement after inheriting part of their grandfather's ranch.

"They want a meeting with Penny as soon as possible," Luke continued.

Caleb shook his head. "That's not going to happen until I can guarantee their safety. Someone connected to this case has obviously been compromised, and I have no reason to trust their agency."

Luke leaned against his desk. "Caleb, a US Marshal was just murdered trying to take Penny and Missy into protective custody. An FBI agent was murdered trying to protect them months ago. The agencies need to question Penny about those incidents."

"She doesn't know anything, Luke."

"You don't know that. You hardly even know this woman."

"I know she's scared and doing everything she can to protect her daughter. If she knew who was after her, she would tell me."

"She might not even realize what she knows," Luke pointed out. "Besides, they're not going to give up until they talk to her and they're certainly not going to take them into protective custody without questioning her."

"That doesn't matter. I'm not so sure witness protection is a good idea right now. Not until we discover how the bad guys found out about the meeting at the diner."

"You think there's some kind of mole working in the Marshals' office?"

"Or the FBI. Or the US Attorney's office. Somehow, these men found out that Marshal Dryer was going to take Penny and Missy into protective custody. I'm sure we weren't followed there so that means the intel had to come from the government's end."

Luke nodded. "We weren't followed. I'm sure of that too." He rubbed his face. "I knew Marissa. She was a good marshal. She would have made certain she wasn't followed either. And even if she was, how would these men have known to follow her? She had no connection to Penny until yesterday. You're right—someone must have fed them information."

"Which means they knew the location of the meet-up ahead of time. They had time to make the bomb and they were ready to place it once she arrived."

He could see Luke was as troubled by this as he was. He nodded. "I'll phone Rose. If there's a leak, she needs to know about it. It's not information she can ignore—even if it comes from me. However, they are still going to insist on speaking with Penny. Two federal agents are dead and she's smack in the middle of it. Plus, they now know that you're involved. I'm surprised they haven't descended on Jessup yet, demanding to know where you're hiding them."

The people running the investigation were probably already digging into his financials, trying to figure out where he might have them stashed. They would start with credit card transactions, looking for hotel charges. When they found nothing, they would move on to properties he owned. He doubted they would find any records of the cabin. It was still technically in his grandfather's name. However, the longer they searched, the more likely it would be that they would locate the cabin in the woods.

It didn't get past him that Luke didn't ask their location. Clearly, his cousin had realized that it was better that he didn't know so he couldn't accidentally give it away to the FBI. Not that Caleb believed he would. Luke was a trained FBI agent and he hadn't been retired so long that he'd forgotten the skills. But, from his own admission, Agent Rose Sinclair was going to be demanding and Caleb couldn't really blame her. She was trying to put away the murderers of two federal agents along with a group of violent bank robbers. And she needed Missy to do so. Caleb was certain that she was going to use every ounce of federal authority in her power to try to find Missy.

If he wanted to keep their location a secret, they were going to have to give her something. "Okay. I'll talk with Penny about setting up a meeting with the FBI but I won't bring Missy along. She'll remain in hiding while the feds are in town."

Luke accepted this compromise. "I'll call Rose and set that up. I agree it's probably better to keep the little girl away. Rose might try something like forcing them into custody. As long as Missy is still out there, she'll play nice. But what will you do with her while Penny is here?"

"I'll think of something." He already had someone in mind to watch the little girl. Someone he trusted more than anyone else in his life, including his cousin.

Luke stood. "I'm heading home to see my wife, then grab a few hours of sleep. I'll let you know when I hear back from Rose."

Luke had spent the night at the crime scene, so Caleb didn't begrudge him getting some rest. There was nothing else any of them could do anyway until he set something up with Rose. But Caleb suddenly realized he was imposing on his cousin's time with his family. "You've already been a huge help to me, Luke. If you'd rather not continue on, I'd understand."

Luke shook his head, determination set in his jaw. "Someone murdered my friend. I want to help find out who did it. Whatever I need to do. I'm in this wholeheartedly." He picked up his jacket and started toward the door, stopping to turn back to Caleb. "Until I hear from Rose, be careful. It's possible the FBI are already in town, watching you to try to get to them."

"I'm sure they'll try but they won't succeed. I'll be careful."

But his cousin was right. Caleb had to be on the look-out for not only the bad guys but also for an FBI tail.

He didn't want to lead anyone to Penny and Missy's location.

Penny awoke with a start, forgetting momentarily where she was. It was a common occurrence these days. She glanced around, reaching for her daughter, her heart racing with fear before calmness set in as she remembered. They were in Caleb's grandfather's fishing cabin. They were safe.

She sat up on the bed and maneuvered around Missy, who was still sleeping. She stood and stretched and glanced out the window at the early morning scene. It was lovely. They were nestled in the woods, surrounded by the sounds of birds chirping. They might have been on vacation instead of running for their lives.

She closed the curtains, shutting out the morning sunlight. Her soul craved it, but safety had to be her first concern. She had no way of knowing when something other than the birds and wildlife might be lurking outside.

She walked into the kitchen and scrounged for something to eat for breakfast, finally settling on a can of chicken noodle soup. Hopefully, Caleb would bring them some bread and other groceries this evening but Missy would be up soon and hungry. This would have to do. They couldn't neglect their nutrition—not when they were already dragging from their chaotic sleep cycle. Another restless night of nightmares had kept them both from a sound sleep. Who was she kidding?

She hadn't had a good night's sleep since this real live nightmare had started. How could she rest knowing that her daughter could be taken or killed at any moment?

She shuddered and turned on the radio. At least, she could have the company of music. It was already tuned to a Christian radio station but the signal was fuzzy. Still, the sound comforted her and kept her from obsessing about every little noise she heard from outside.

She grabbed the can of soup, opened it and heated it up on the stove. Missy stumbled into the room as she was pouring it into two bowls. She rubbed her eyes and, for a moment, Penny thought she was going to smile and say, "Hi, Mama," the way she used to. Oh, how she wanted her to, but instead she only pulled back a chair and stared at Penny with a dullness in her eyes.

"Good morning, sweetheart."

Penny turned away, doing her best to choke back the tears that threatened her. She missed the cheerful little girl her daughter used to be. She wanted that girl back.

She pasted on a smile as she handed Missy a bowl and was glad to see her eat something. Even her appetite had become off lately with all the stress of the trauma she'd witnessed and all the running they'd been doing.

The cell phone Caleb had given her buzzed on the cabinet and her heart jumped at the sound. Although she knew only one person had this number, fear still rumbled through her at the prospect of it being anyone else.

She reached for it and answered before she allowed fear to take her over. "Hello?"

"Good morning."

She couldn't stop the smile that spread across her

face at the familiar bass and texture of Caleb's voice. "Good morning."

"Did I wake you?"

"No, we've been up for a while. I just finished fixing Missy something to eat."

"Good. I'll bring some more groceries by this afternoon when I come."

"Thank you. I'd appreciate that."

"If you need to reach me, use this number. It's untraceable. I know I don't have to tell you this but stay close to the cabin today. Don't venture out unless you have to. I'm certain it's safe enough but I don't want to risk anyone seeing you."

"Don't worry about us. We've become pros at staying hidden." Her heart clenched at the truth in that statement. Only, they hadn't been good enough. They'd been found.

"Luke is in contact with someone from the FBI. They have questions about what happened with the marshal."

"Will we have to go and get questioned by them?" Fear struck her again. She wanted to trust the FBI but after what had happened last night, she wasn't sure she could.

"We may have to, but I don't think it's a good idea to let Missy near them until we know how the marshal was compromised. If there's a leak in one of the agencies, I won't risk yours and Missy's safety."

She felt better knowing that Caleb was looking out for them. She'd become so used to not trusting anyone in law enforcement that she didn't understand how she could trust him, yet she did. He'd been there for them ever since that first day, looking out for their safety and asking for nothing in return.

Who did that?

He promised to see them later that day, then ended the call.

She turned to see that Missy had finished her soup and had gone to the living room to play with an old box of Legos stashed in the corner. Caleb had said this was his grandfather's fishing cabin and that he and his cousins used to come here with him and their dads all the time. The toys must be leftovers from those days. She was grateful they were there since it gave Missy something to do other than coloring more gruesome pictures.

There was also a television with a DVD player and a cabinet of old movies. Perhaps they could find something to watch later. Anything to take their minds off their troubles.

Otherwise, Penny knew how she would be spending her day—trying to figure a way out of the mess they'd found themselves in.

# SIX

Caleb arranged to have groceries delivered to his house, then sent a text to Hannah, Harmon Ranch's house-keeper for as long as he could remember, to have the bags loaded into one of the ranch's pickups. He intended to drive up to the fishing cabin after he left the office and he wanted to be as inconspicuous as possible.

His instincts were on high alert and he had to make sure he didn't lead anyone to the cabin where Penny and Missy were hiding out.

He finished up paperwork that needed to be ad-dressed, then checked out with Dispatch early, letting them know to only call him in an emergency for the rest of the afternoon and evening. For everything else, his deputy chief could handle it while he was out.

He climbed into his SUV and drove through town, looking for anyone or anything that was out of place or didn't belong in his town. Whether FBI or criminals, he knew he wouldn't hesitate to pull someone over if he didn't recognize them. The bad guys knew Penny and Missy had come here. They'd already tried to kill them more than once. And he didn't trust that the FBI wasn't sniffing around town too.

Caleb wasn't taking any chances.

He stopped at a café and ordered a coffee and a couple of sandwiches, taking the time to chat with several of the regulars as he waited for his food to be prepared.

A group of men usually met up at the café on a regular basis and Caleb knew they kept up with the comings and goings of the town. They'd been good witnesses on several cases and he was hoping their eagle eyes would have spotted anything in the area that might be out of the ordinary.

Every small town had a group of people who were the eyes and ears of the community. Sometimes they could be a nuisance, especially when outsiders had legitimate reasons to be in town, but other times they could be the first line of defense against intruders. He was hoping this group would alert him to the criminal strangers in town before they could do any more damage.

He approached the back booth where they always sat. "How's it going, fellows?"

They all nodded at him. "Chief," Mac Harlow greeted him.

"You guys seen or heard anything good lately?"

They all shook their heads.

"What about anyone unfamiliar in town? Seen anyone?"

"I've seen a few strange cars roaming around lately," Shelton Bird stated. "Looked like Dallas tags to me."

Several of the other men nodded.

"I'd be very interested in those," Caleb told him. "If

you see them again, will you call them in to the police station?"

"You all looking for someone?" Mac asked.

"Just making sure people who are in town aren't looking for trouble."

"Will do, Chief."

The barista called his name and he walked over to retrieve his coffee and sandwiches. As he was paying, he noticed a display of cookies and thought Penny and Missy might like to have a treat. "Wrap up two of those to go with the sandwiches, please," he told her. Then he paid, took his items and walked back to his SUV. He headed for the ranch and, once he arrived, he hurried upstairs to change before going down to the garage. He was glad to see Hannah had done as he'd asked and the groceries were loaded on the front floorboard. He could always count on her. He added the sandwiches and cookies into the bags, then headed off the ranch using the back exit, heading north toward the fishing cabin.

Caleb had his eyes glued to his mirrors for any signs that he was being followed but he saw no other vehicles on the road as he drove. His mind was running through all the scenarios of how he could best keep Penny and Missy safe, but he still had nothing aside from keeping them hidden as he turned off the highway and onto the dirt road that led up to the cabin.

He parked and got out, still searching and scanning the area for anything wrong or out of place. He saw nothing but he still wasn't letting his guard down. The men after Penny and Missy could be anywhere and they had already made it clear that they weren't giving up anytime soon.

He grabbed the groceries, then used his key to let himself inside the cabin before he closed and locked the door behind him.

Missy was stretched out on the floor, watching a video on the TV, but Penny was asleep on the couch.

Missy gave him a wave and he waved back. "Hey there."

At the sound of his voice, Penny jerked up, instantly on alert.

"It's okay," he told her, seeing the fear on her face. "It's just me, Caleb."

But his arrival clearly had her shaken. Her eyes were wide with fear and her breathing heavy as she clutched her chest. "I can't believe you drove up and came inside and I didn't even hear you."

He understood. As much as she wanted to be on alert, she had to be completely exhausted. He wondered when the last time she'd felt safe enough to sleep soundly had been. He guessed it had been a while and it was finally catching up with her.

"It's okay," he assured her. "You're safe."

His reassurance didn't seem to soothe her. She jumped to her feet, gave Missy a quick glance, then hurried to help him with the bags of groceries. She took one bag from his hand and started unloading it. Yet he could see her mind whirling with thoughts.

"You have to give yourself a break," he told her.

She leaned against the counter. "If I give myself a

break, it might be the last one. It might be the opening they need to get to her."

She wasn't wrong, but she also wasn't super woman with unending strength. Stubbornness alone wouldn't make up for the clarity that could only come from deep sleep. He'd been on stakeouts with little to no sleep and he knew the effects it had on a person's physical and mental capacities.

"Penny, you can't keep going like this without rest. You won't make it."

"What choice do I have?"

He touched her arm and forced her to look at him. "You have a choice now. You can trust me." He wanted her trust so badly. He couldn't even say why, but it was important to him. Yet, her eyes still held doubts. Uncertainty. She was holding back from trusting him completely and it stung him. All he wanted to do was keep her safe. "I'll stay here tonight on the couch and stand guard. You and Missy can get some real sleep for once. I promise you that no one will get to you while I'm here."

He saw her struggling with the decision but she needed this and he was willing to provide it. He took her arm. "Penny, nothing will happen to you or Missy as long as I'm here. What can I do to prove that to you?"

She shrugged, then gave him a sorrowful look. "You've already done more than enough to prove yourself to me, Caleb. I want to let my guard down, but I'm just not good at trusting people. Maybe if it were just me, it wouldn't be so difficult, but I have to think about Missy too and it's so much harder to rely on anyone else when it comes to her."

He understood and even admired her a little bit more for her prudence. Every choice and decision she made was weighed first and foremost by how it could affect Missy. She was a good mom, devoted to her daughter. That was the way it should be. Not like his own mother who hadn't bothered to stick around long enough to see him settled into his grandfather's ranch before she'd skipped town again. He saw her only a handful of times after he'd come to live in Jessup. She would pop in occasionally and always sent him birthday and Christmas cards with money tucked inside.

As if that made up for her abandonment.

He felt his own jaw clench at the memory. He'd needed a mother, not a bank account.

But Penny had sacrificed everything for her daughter and that determination spurred Caleb to make certain they were safe. Part of that included making sure she was clearheaded in the way that she could only be after getting some real rest.

He reached for her hands and held them. "Penny, you don't know me that well but you need to know that I will do whatever it takes to keep you and your daughter out of harm's way. I know it's difficult but I'm asking you to put some faith in me. I promise you that I will protect your daughter with the very last breath of my own life."

She squirmed under his gaze and tried to pull her hands away. She was still hesitant but he could tell she was coming to realize what she'd already admitted—she needed to trust someone.

She bit her lip, then nodded her agreement. "I'll try."

It was enough. Giving up control was a difficult

thing. He knew that as well as anybody. Now that she was handing over a little of that control to him, he was determined not to let her down.

She picked up a can of tomato sauce. "At least we can have a good meal first, right?"

"Sure."

His grocery order had been based on stocking up, so aside from a few perishable items—bread, milk, eggs and lettuce—most of their food came in a can or box. He used the nonelectric can opener on a can of spaghetti sauce while she boiled pasta and made a simple salad. It wasn't much but it was good.

Missy picked at her food for a few minutes before curling up on the couch with her stuffed monkey to watch a movie.

Penny's mouth twisted with worry. "She didn't eat much. Maybe she will finish it later."

"It was good even if I did have a hand in making it. It's been a while since I've done much cooking," he confessed, pleased when she pressed a hand against her mouth to conceal a giggle.

"You still haven't done much cooking," she teased. "Heating something out of a can doesn't count as cooking. If we were at my house, I would make you homemade sauce from my mother's recipe, fresh pasta and biscuits made from scratch." Her eyes glowed with excitement for a moment before becoming downcast again.

"Sounds good. Our housekeeper at Harmon Ranch makes sure we have meals in the freezer and she cooks a big Sunday dinner every week for the family and all the ranch employees. Other than her cooking, I exist mainly on takeout—and heating up stuff from a can. It fits my lifestyle."

"I love to cook. Being a single mom, money was always tight, but my mom taught me how to stretch a food budget through home cooking." Her face showed weariness. "I miss her. She died from cancer when I was sixteen."

"I'm sorry. I know what it's like to lose a parent. My father was killed in a car accident when I was twelve. I miss him. What about your father?"

"I never knew him. He left my mother when I was a baby and was never a part of my life. She was the only family I had. I lived with friends off and on until I graduated from high school."

"How long has it just been you and Missy?" He watched her to see if his question was too personal, but he was curious where Missy's father was in all of this and why he wasn't stepping up to protect his family. This seemed like a natural segue in the conversation.

She grimaced but answered him. "My husband, Missy's father, was killed in a bar fight three years ago but, truthfully, I don't think he would have been much help to us in this situation. Devon was a very self-absorbed person. I met him during a time in my life when I was young and very lonely. There were a lot of red flags which I completely ignored because he claimed to love me. It wasn't until I had Missy that I even realized how badly he treated us. He drank, did drugs, gambled and would disappear for weeks at a time. He completely shirked his responsibilities to his family. I was sorry when he died but my life got a lot less complicated…until now that is."

So she too knew what it felt like to be abandoned by those who were supposed to protect her. For her, it had been her father and husband. For him, his mother. Only, instead of shutting down like he'd done, she'd chosen to be everything for her child.

He'd shied away from getting too serious with anyone or even entertaining the idea of becoming a parent because of the way he'd been hurt. The way she gave so openly to her daughter mesmerized him.

She was truly an amazing woman.

They left the dishes for later and joined Missy for one movie, then another as the sky outside the windows grew dark. It was a quiet night with just the three of them and the glow of the TV. He liked it. It was simple and peaceful and just what they needed to wind down.

He glanced over at Penny and saw Missy asleep in her arms, her stuffed toy clutched to her chest. The child looked so peaceful that he hated to disturb her, but he saw Penny growing uncomfortable with the awkward position.

"Do you want me to move her into the bedroom?"

"Please."

Caleb lifted the child easily into his arms and she didn't squirm as he carried her. Penny pulled back the blankets so he could lay Missy on the bed, then covered her for warmth. She leaned over and kissed her daughter's cheek as Caleb stood at the door and watched the scene.

It struck him as honest and sincere and touched him.

Who had ever showed him such care before? Only Hannah, who'd done her best to be a surrogate mother to him. It hadn't been easy either. He'd been an angry, resentful child, full of bitterness and mayhem. He'd only managed to pull his life together as a young adult after being arrested by the former chief of police for drag racing through the town square.

He walked back into the kitchen and ran water into the sink to wash the supper dishes.

Moments later, Penny appeared beside him, picked up a towel and began drying. They worked in silence for several minutes until they'd finished washing the last plate. "Thank you for tonight, Caleb. I think this was the first time in weeks that we've had time to unwind and just enjoy ourselves without being worried about what might happen next."

"I'm glad."

"I do want to trust you."

"It's okay," he assured her. "It's a work in progress."

"I do believe I'll sleep better tonight knowing that you're here. At least, I hope I will."

"It's understandable that you would have trouble sleeping."

She nodded, looking sad and weary. "I have such terrible nightmares and then I wake up so frightened at what might have happened while I was sleeping." A tear slid down her cheek and she discreetly wiped it away. "I don't know what we're going to do, Caleb. I don't see a way out of this."

"Don't talk like that. We'll figure it out."

"After what happened to the marshal, I'm so afraid

they're going to find us again. I just don't know why this all had to happen. Why did I have to go to that bank on that day?"

"There's no sense in questioning why. It happened. That's all that matters. But this isn't the end for you, Penny. There's a way out of this and we will find it. You have to have faith."

She cringed at his mention of faith but tried to hide it by lowering her head and focusing on putting away the plates she'd just toweled off.

"You don't believe in God?"

"No, I do. I mean, I'm trying to. Faith was my life raft for a long time. I trusted God to take care of us even in the darkest days when my husband would abuse me. I even trusted Him to find us a way out of this mess when it first happened. After the agent was killed, everything just got worse and I just don't know what to believe in anymore." She tossed the towel onto the counter and turned away from him. Her shoulders shook as she sobbed.

He struggled to find words that would bring her comfort but knew nothing he could say would really do any good.

"Faith is what we cling to when everything else seems lost," he told her. "I understand how it can be difficult to have faith when everything around you seems to be falling apart, but Jeremiah 29:11 says that God has plans for our lives and that they are good plans—not for harm but for good. I have to cling to that whenever I can't see the answers to my problems. I can't explain

God's plans, but I trust that they're good because I trust in Him."

She turned back to look at him, her lashes wet with tears. "I'm having a difficult time with that lately."

He reached out to wipe a tear from her cheek and felt her lean her face into his hand. "Hey, I'm here with you now. You and Missy are not alone in this any longer. Have faith in that."

"I'll try." She leaned up and kissed his cheek. "I think I'll turn in now." She walked to the bedroom door, then turned back to look at him. "Good night."

"Sleep well." Once she'd closed the door, Caleb touched his cheek where her lips had touched him. That had caught him off guard.

It sent his mind wandering to a place he'd always purposefully avoided—a future with a family.

He'd never seen himself as a family man. In fact, he'd made a point of guarding his heart to avoid that very thing and spare himself the heartbreak of getting hurt.

He'd watched his cousin reconnect with Abby, the woman who'd broken his heart when they were just kids, and he saw how happy they were together. It was like a cold wake-up call that he too needed to take a chance. Having Luke and Abby's happy family in front of him was a constant sting, reminding him that he didn't have the same thing.

He didn't blame them and he was glad they were happy. He simply didn't understand how his cousin had gotten past his anger and forgiven Abby for her deception. And, more importantly, he didn't understand how he was supposed to take a chance on love when his instinct was to pull away the moment his heart might get involved. It was an ingrained response in him and one he'd never been able to get past.

Hannah had told him his choice of dates was another reason he had a difficult time finding someone he could build a future with. He tended to choose women who were inherently shallow, thereby proving his point that all women would eventually break his heart.

He glanced at the closed bedroom door. He couldn't classify Penny Jackson that way. He'd never before met such a selfless woman.

He shook off those feelings. If he could ever see himself going down that road, it would be with someone like Penny, but he couldn't allow himself that luxury. Not with her. Given everything she was dealing with, he was certain that romance was the last thing on her mind. Everything in her was focused on caring for and protecting her daughter. She had no time for anything else. Besides, if things went right, she would be entering WITSEC and he would never see her again. Her situation was designed to break his heart if he got too attached.

He sighed and rubbed his face. He was feeling sorry for himself when what he needed to do was figure out who was after Penny and Missy and how to stop them. He pulled out his laptop and scanned through the notes he and Luke had made about the case. They still hadn't identified the two men who had attacked Penny the other night—or the man who had planted the bomb.

The FBI were working through all the robbers' known associates and had provided Luke with that information despite Luke's concern that Agent Sinclair wouldn't share her intel. Caleb has issued an alert for each of those men in the department and publicly, saying that he wanted to know about any outsiders. If any one of them was in town, he'd hopefully get word about it right away.

But Caleb knew what the FBI really wanted was Penny and Missy's location. They wanted to take them into protective custody but he wasn't sure that was such a good idea, at least not until the circumstances surrounding the marshal's murder were cleared up. How had the assailants discovered where they were going to be? How had they known to be at that diner at that moment? If these guys could penetrate the FBI or the Marshals' security, then that meant Penny and Missy couldn't be safe with them until those questions were answered and the leak was plugged.

Those were the issues that whirled through his mind as he dozed on the sofa, one ear on alert for any sign of intruders. There were none and, as the sun rose and light beamed through the corners of the window coverings, he got up to stoke the fire. It was a chilly spring morning and he knew Penny and Missy would be getting up soon. He wanted the cabin to be warm. They hadn't stirred much throughout the night so he hoped that meant they'd both slept soundly. That would make a world of difference in their attitudes and emotions.

His cell phone buzzed. He picked it up and saw a text message from Luke. The FBI had arrived in Jessup and were demanding that meeting with Penny.

He'd expected them to arrive but not so soon. He

hadn't had a chance to get Penny comfortable with the idea yet.

He shot off another text message to make arrangements for Missy. He wasn't allowing her anywhere near the FBI until he could assure her safety. He received a quick response to his text with an agreement to watch Missy while he and Penny dealt with the feds.

He sighed and put away his phone. It was time to wake them up, then to do his best to convince Penny that separating from Missy for a little while was the best plan. She wouldn't want to leave her daughter's side, but she was going to have to in order to keep the little girl safe.

Penny's hands shook as she poured herself a glass of milk. Everything Caleb had explained about meeting with the FBI made sense, but that didn't make it less scary.

He watched her, waiting for her to agree to the meeting. She didn't want to. She preferred to remain here at the cabin—safe from the outside world.

He must have seen that because he pressed her again. "I've got people in town that want to know what happened. They're demanding answers about why a US Marshal is dead."

Penny rubbed her face and breathed out a frustrated sigh. "I don't know anything. I don't know how they found us."

He reached for her hand and held it, doing his best to reassure her. "And that's exactly what you'll tell them."

"It won't be enough for them."

"It'll have to be."

"Don't you get it, Caleb? It's never enough. They want answers but I don't have any and I won't be bullied and harassed by them again. All they want is to put my daughter's life in danger."

"I won't allow that to happen, Penny. You have to trust me," he said. His words reminded her of last night, when she'd promised to try. But that fragile, open moment felt long gone now, and this time, she lashed out at him.

"Trust you? I hardly know you. How do I know you aren't just like them?"

He didn't say anything and she turned to look at him. His expression was one of sadness, disappointment and—more than that—hurt by her accusation. "I'm sorry," she said. She did trust Caleb more than any law enforcement officer she'd ever met, but right now, her faith had limits. She'd placed her daughter's life in his hands. How did she know she could really trust him?

He put his hands on his hips and blew out a sigh, then approached her. "If you couldn't trust me, Penny, you and your daughter would already be in the hands of the FBI. I made a choice that first day we met. I received the BOLO on you and Missy and I could have called them in to pick you both up right away. If I'd done that, then I'd have spared myself all this frustration and heartache. But I didn't. I saw two people in trouble and I wanted to help. You have every right to wonder if the people you're placing your lives in the hands of can be relied on to put you first instead of focusing on their own agendas. But I hope you know I'm on your side.

I don't have a stake in any of this except to see you're both all right."

He *didn't* have a stake, which made his helping them all the stranger. "Why did you stick your neck out then?"

He shook his head. "My cousin asked me that too."

"I'd really like to know."

At first, it seemed like he wasn't going to tell her, but then he moved toward her. "I didn't have a great relationship with my own mother. She was selfish and narcissistic. I've had to learn to live with the fact that I got a raw deal in the maternal department. So when I saw how fiercely you were fighting for Missy, I knew I wanted to help you. That's it. That's my only reason for being here."

She didn't understand that. "I was only doing what any mother would do."

He shook his head. "You're wrong. Not every mother would sacrifice so much to protect their child. Some mothers wouldn't do a fraction of what you have. I've seen it. I've experienced it. You're a good mom and I only want to help you."

She had a difficult time believing she was a good mom. She certainly didn't feel like it. In fact, she felt like she was anything but. She'd managed to mess this all up. She'd been the one to take Missy to the bank that day, then she'd been fooled by the FBI and bullied into letting her daughter become a target. How could anyone see her as a good mother?

He looked at her again. "For now, we've got to go and face these agents. You'll tell them just what you've said to me—that you don't know anything. The fact that the marshal was killed wasn't your fault. They need to check their systems. Someone alerted them to our meeting and it wasn't us."

She nodded, then took a deep breath. "I don't want to go but, if you say we have to, I will. As long as you're there with us."

He grimaced. "I'll be there with *you*, definitely—but that's another thing. I don't think it's a good idea to bring Missy. They'll want to question her. They might even use some legal tactic to try to take her into protective custody without your consent."

Her heart raced. "You think they'll try to take her away from me?" She hadn't even considered they might try that.

"I wouldn't put it past them. I texted Hannah, my housekeeper. She can watch Missy for a few hours while we meet with the feds."

Suddenly, all the air left her lungs and Penny couldn't catch her breath. "I can't leave her. I can't be without her."

He knelt beside her and kept his voice low and steady. "Listen to me, Penny. Trust me. Hannah can handle herself. If anyone tries to harm Missy, they'll have to go through her first."

"I haven't been away from her in months. She hasn't left my side."

"I know. And I know you're scared, but this is what's best for her. We have to go meet with the feds. It's better if she's not with you when you do. It gives us some leverage."

Everything he was saying was true, yet Penny couldn't stand the thought of being away from Missy even for a few hours. She'd spent every moment for the past months watching out for her and, now, Caleb was asking her to leave her behind. Even though it was only for a short while, it still felt like he was trying to rip her away.

She got control of her breathing. She couldn't allow panic to cloud her judgment. Caleb was right. Having Missy with her around the FBI would only serve their purposes and she wouldn't put it past them to try to take her. They were determined to make their case no matter how it affected Missy.

She looked up at him, took a deep breath and nodded. "Okay. If you trust Hannah, then okay."

He smiled. "I promise you—Hannah can take care of her. And it's only for a little while."

She was still nervous about leaving Missy with anyone, but she'd made a decision to trust Caleb and she had to stick with it. She certainly trusted him far more than she trusted anyone with the FBI.

# SEVEN

After breakfast, she bundled Missy up and loaded her into Caleb's truck. She was nervous about being back out in the open, especially in the daytime when someone could see them, but that was nothing to how she felt about leaving Missy behind even for an hour or two.

He drove back toward town but turned off before they hit the city limits.

"I asked Hannah if we could bring Missy to her house. The feds might suspect y'all are at the ranch or start looking into places I own, but they have no reason to suspect Hannah. And even if they do look into her, the house originally belonged to her late husband and it's still in his name."

She tried her best to settle down, but he must have noticed her nervousness. He slid his hand across the seat and held hers. It helped. His grip reminded her that he was strong and capable of protecting them. He was on their side and it felt good to have someone on their side. It wasn't something she'd ever really had before.

Her face warmed at the memory of the kiss she'd given him last night. It had been spontaneous and obviously caught them both off guard but she wasn't sorry. She'd wanted a way to thank him and a kiss had seemed the most appropriate way to show her gratitude.

Never mind that she'd spent the rest of the night thinking about the weight of his hands on hers and the scent of his aftershave.

"Here we are." He turned into the driveway of a ranch-style house, then drove around to the back of it.

A fresh wave of nervousness struck her. "What is Hannah like?"

"She's amazing. She's worked for my family for as long as I can remember and has been more like a mother to me than my own mother ever was. Don't worry. She'll take good care of Missy."

Caleb parked, then shut off the engine and jumped out. He circled around the truck as Penny unbuckled Missy and made certain she had her stuffed monkey and her crayons for drawing. Penny prayed her daughter didn't draw anything too upsetting while she was with Hannah and they were gone.

Caleb led them through the back door where they were greeted by a woman with short, graying hair and a wide smile. She threw her arms around Caleb and he hugged her back.

"Hannah, this is Penny."

Penny reached to shake her hand. "It's nice to meet you, Penny. I've heard a lot about you from Caleb."

"Nice to meet you too," Penny said.

Caleb motioned to Missy. "This is Penny's daughter, Missy. She's the one I told you about."

Hannah knelt down and shook Missy's hand. "It's nice to meet you, Missy."

"She doesn't talk," Penny said, feeling the need to explain her lack of communication.

Hannah seemed unfazed by it and didn't even question why a child of her age didn't speak. "That's okay. We'll find a way to communicate, won't we, sweetheart?"

She reached out her hand and Missy took it and followed her into the living room. The fact that Missy seemed to trust her spoke volumes.

"We hopefully won't be gone long," Caleb explained, "but when you're dealing with the FBI you can never really say."

"Don't worry about it," Hannah insisted. "I wasn't planning on going anywhere. Take your time. We'll be just fine."

After meeting Hannah, Penny felt better about leaving Missy with her. She seemed to be a nice woman who had real affection for Caleb. Seeing that maternal side of her put Penny at ease. She knelt down and gave Missy a hug. "You mind Miss Hannah and be a good girl until I get back. Okay?"

Missy nodded, then followed Hannah into the kitchen while Caleb placed his hands on Penny's shoulders.

"She's going to be okay," he reassured her. She wanted to believe him. She *needed* to believe him. But walking away from her daughter was the hardest thing she'd done.

She pressed her hands to her cheeks to try to force back the swell of tears that threatened to spill out at the idea of leaving Missy. That was only her fear and she couldn't allow it to control her.

They got back into the pickup and Caleb turned to look at her before starting the engine. "Are you ready to face this?"

She took a deep breath as she struggled to gain control of her emotions. "I'm ready," she told him. The truth was that she didn't have much choice but to be ready. The FBI was going to find them no matter what she did. She had to face this head-on.

Caleb felt the tension flowing off of Penny as he drove toward the police station. Luke was waiting for them there, along with Agent Rose Sinclair of the FBI and someone from the US Marshals' office. Caleb had already been alerted by text that several locals had called into Dispatch, warning about the out-of-town vehicles.

He didn't want to put Penny through this but the FBI and Marshals' office would not go away without asking their questions. Although he didn't believe Penny would be able to offer them any answers, a marshal had lost her life and that needed to be investigated.

He parked, then took her hand and squeezed it. "We can get through this."

She looked at him and took in a deep breath. "I'm ready."

They entered through the back entrance and met Luke and the others in the conference room. He held open the door for Penny, who walked in in front of him.

A woman with long dark hair and professional clothes and manner approached them. "Penny, I've been so worried."

"You two know each other?" Caleb asked.

Penny nodded. "Agent Sinclair was the agent in charge of investigating the bank robbery."

"And Missy is our star witness." She glanced around them. "Where is she?"

"She's not here," Penny explained. "We thought it would be better to leave her somewhere safe."

Agent Sinclair's mouth twisted unhappily but Penny didn't back down. In fact, she stood up straighter and faced the agent unabashed.

"You wanted to question me about the marshal's death and Missy had nothing to do with that. There was no reason why she'd be needed, so we left her behind. My main concern is keeping my daughter safe."

Agent Sinclair folded her arms and locked eyes with Penny in a confrontational manner. "And you don't think we can keep her safe?"

Caleb thought she was trying to intimidate Penny but, once again, Penny refused to back down.

"So far, neither of you have done a great job with that. First the break-in at the hotel and now the marshal. Forgive me if I have doubts about your ability to protect us."

Caleb bit back a grin, his admiration for this woman continuing to grow. She was scared for sure, but she wasn't a wilting flower to be pushed around and he was glad to see that part of her emerge. Her strength of spirit amazed him.

Luke spotted him grinning and shook his head, a warning not to get too cocky with Agent Sinclair. Since Luke knew her better than Caleb did, the police chief took the hint and forced himself into a more neutral expression.

Agent Sinclair turned to the man standing on the other side of the conference room table. "This is Marshal David Kirk. He was Marshal Dryer's supervisor."

Caleb and Penny both shook his extended hand.

"We're very sorry about Marshal Dryer," Caleb told him. "My cousin spoke very fondly of her and even though I only got to meet her briefly, she seemed like a nice person."

"Thank you. She was an exceptional marshal. We're very anxious to uncover who killed her."

"So are we. I'll tell you, I know we were not followed to the meeting. I was watching to make certain. Plus, I had my cousin following behind us. However they learned about the meet-up, it wasn't on our end."

"You're saying it was on us then?" Agent Sinclair demanded.

"I know how to spot a tail," Luke told her. "You know I do. No one followed us to the meet-up."

Agent Sinclair turned to Caleb and Penny. "Who did you tell about the meeting?"

"No one outside my office even knew about Penny and Missy," Caleb insisted. "And no one except Luke was privy to the location of the meeting."

"I'm still going to want to perform background checks on all your staff."

Caleb wasn't worried about his staff and was certain no one in his office had any connection to the people targeting Penny and Missy. "That's fine. Are you also investigating your own agents?"

"I'll be performing an investigation into my office," Marshal Kirk stated. "Given that we lost one of our own in the bombing, I need to ensure our security measures haven't been compromised."

Agent Sinclair sighed. "I'm certain no one in my office leaked the information. However, we will be conducting an in-house investigation as well, just to be thorough. I'll make sure the AG's office does too. I don't want to believe that any law enforcement agency is compromised, although I have to admit, this criminal organization seems to have been one step ahead of us for a long time."

That bothered him to hear. It sounded like there had been a leak in Agent Sinclair's organization for quite a while. "Until you suss out the mole, you can't guarantee Penny and Missy's safety within your system of protections. That's already been proven. But they can stay here until it's safe to move them."

"I don't think that's a good idea," Agent Sinclair stated. "They've already been targeted here in Jessup by unknown assailants. Now that the others have been released, they'll probably be heading here too. The only way those men can stay out of prison is by making sure Missy can never testify against them."

He saw that her words frightened Penny and was sure that was Agent Sinclair's intention. The agent wanted Penny frightened so that she would hopefully come to her for protection.

He moved beside Penny to reassure her as he refuted Sinclair's assumption. "The fact that Jessup is a small town works in our favor. Strangers stand out like a sore thumb." In fact, that was the reason Penny and Missy first came on his radar—he'd noticed them, even before the almost hit-and-run, because he hadn't recognized them. "I've got roadblocks in place and my officers are all on high alert. If these men show up in our town, we'll know about it. Besides, I've got Penny and Missy well hidden. No one is going to uncover their location."

Agent Sinclair's mouth twisted again as if she knew his statement was true, even if she didn't like it. He suspected she'd been trying to figure out where he'd hidden them with no success. She wouldn't stop trying, convinced the FBI and marshals could protect Penny and Missy better than he could. He might have once agreed that was true if they didn't suspect there was a mole hidden somewhere in their organizations.

Agent Sinclair looked at Penny. "Is that what you want too?"

Penny nodded. "I trust Caleb, and I believe he's right. Until you find out how these men are discovering our location, my daughter isn't safe with you. I feel better remaining with Caleb until then."

He beamed from her vote of confidence. "It's settled then. We'll keep in touch with you through Luke. Once you've uncovered the source of the leak—and only then—Penny and Missy enter witness protection. Until then, I'll keep them hidden and safe."

"And what if you can't? What if these men somehow find them again?"

Luke stepped forward. "Then we'll take care of it together."

She glared at Luke, then at Caleb, looking like she

wanted to say more, but she held back—probably able to see that it would be useless. Finally, she turned to Marshal Kirk. "We should go." She turned back to them. "We'll be in touch soon." She stopped to address Penny. "I still have your signed agreement that Missy will testify against this group. It's a binding agreement and we expect you to keep it."

He didn't care for the veiled threat but Penny seemed unbothered by it.

"My only concern is keeping my daughter safe."

Agent Sinclair and Marshal Kirk left. Caleb didn't breathe a relieved sigh until they were in their vehicle and headed out of town.

He took Penny's hands. "Thank you for having confidence in me. I won't let you down."

He'd no sooner said the words than Officer Tim James entered the conference room. "Chief, we have a problem."

"What happened?"

"It's Carl."

His heart squeezed. Carl Joiner was the officer he'd posted to stand guard at Hannah's while he and Penny met with the feds. "What happened?"

"He phoned in a suspicious vehicle. Then his radio cut out. Since then, he's not responding to calls."

Joiner was reliable, and if he wasn't responding that meant something was wrong.

Caleb's heart hammered. He glanced over at Penny and saw realization hit her. "We have to get over there now." He called for several officers to follow him, then headed for the door. Luke was also at his heels and he realized Penny was following him too. He turned at the car and stopped her, trying to lead her back inside. "You need to stay here where it's safe."

She pulled her arm away from his grip. "I'm coming. If Missy is in trouble, I want to be there."

"I don't know what we're walking into here, Penny."

"I'm coming." She put her hands on her hips and gave him that determined stare he'd admired just minutes earlier when she'd used it on Agent Sinclair. It wasn't nearly as fun to have it trained on him.

He didn't have time to argue and, truthfully, he was glad to keep her in his sights. But he worried about what they might find when they reached Hannah's. His gut clenched at the thought. He'd promised her that Hannah could keep her daughter safe. And what if Hannah herself had been hurt? How could he ever forgive himself if she was harmed because she'd wanted to help him? "Get in but stay close to me."

He turned on the sirens and raced toward Hannah's place at the edge of town. Three cruisers followed behind him and he knew his cousin was inside one of them. He reached for the radio and tried to reach Joiner himself.

No answer.

That didn't bode well. His officer would respond if he were able.

Caleb grabbed his cell phone and hit the button to dial Hannah's number. The ringing of the phone filled the car but she didn't pick up.

Also not good. Something must have happened to Hannah for her not to be answering the phone.

He gripped the steering wheel tighter and stole a glance at Penny beside him. She was stiff and tense—and she had every right to be. Had he let her down?

He pulled to a stop in front of Hannah's house, then hopped out. Joiner's police cruiser was there with the door hanging open. Joiner himself was nowhere in sight.

"Stay in the car," Caleb told Penny. Then he drew his weapon and hurried to the front door. It was standing open too.

He stepped inside. The house was quiet—quieter than he'd ever remembered it being. Hannah was usually in the kitchen cooking or baking and she always hummed to herself as she did so. He heard no humming today. He motioned for his team to spread out and search the house. He headed through to the kitchen and saw evidence of food being prepared and spilled milk dripping from the counter to the floor from an overturned cup.

*God, please let them be unharmed.*

He moved into the family room and stumbled upon a body lying on the floor beside the couch. Joiner. He knelt beside him, relieved when he felt a pulse. He was merely unconscious but Caleb couldn't help but notice his weapon was missing from its holster—and it didn't appear to be on the floor anywhere.

Luke and two officers appeared in the doorway, guns drawn. Their eyes widened when they spotted Joiner.

"He's alive," Caleb told them. "Call for an ambulance while I search the back of the house."

"I'm coming too," Luke stated.

Caleb nodded, then raised his gun again as he moved down the hallway to where the bedrooms were located.

His heart hammered at what he might find but he did his best to tamp down those thoughts. Jumping to conclusions would help no one. He and Luke cleared two spare rooms before entering Hannah's primary suite. His gaze swept the room. It was empty.

He moved to the attached bathroom. Also empty.

He turned back to his cousin and shook his head.

Suddenly, the light seemed to glint off of something from the closet, grabbing his attention. He spun and raised his gun as he approached the closet door.

He pulled it open and took aim, only to find himself face-to-face with a rifle barrel. Hannah was crouched on the floor, rifle in hand, while Missy clung to her from behind.

They both relaxed at the same moment and lowered their weapons. "Hannah, what happened?"

"Someone tried to get inside the house so we hid in the closet. I could have taken them down but my first responsibility was to protect the little girl."

Caleb knew her well enough to know her overconfidence was blustering to cover her fear. She knew how to use that rifle and she would have if confronted, but she'd made the right choice by hiding. Protecting Missy had been the most important thing and she'd done that.

"Missy!"

He spun around to see Penny run into the room. Missy hurried to her, and Penny scooped her daughter up. Missy clung to her mother.

"She's perfectly fine," Hannah assured her as Caleb helped her to her feet. "Just a little shaken up."

Caleb pulled her aside. "Did you see the person who broke in?"

"No. Officer Joiner claimed to see someone sneaking around the house. He phoned me and told me to hide while he checked it out. I didn't hear anything more until I heard you walking around. Where is he? Did he find the intruder?"

"We found Joiner knocked out in the living room. Maybe, once he's conscious, we'll get some answers. The intruder, whoever he was, is long gone." He checked Hannah for any injuries. "Are you hurt?"

"No, I'm fine. And Missy's fine too." Hannah turned to Penny again. "No one got to her. I promise."

Penny looked up from where she was wrapped around her daughter and mouthed a *thank you* to Hannah.

Luke hurried back into the room. "The rest of the house is clear and there's no one in sight, but I spoke to a neighbor who saw someone darting out the back minutes before we arrived. We're tracking him now."

"Can they identify him?" If it was one of the men who'd attacked Penny at her house, then this would be confirmation that they hadn't left town.

"Not really. She only saw a figure. She didn't get a good look at him."

Hannah spoke up. "We have security cameras at the front and back doors. They might have captured him. I can pull up those images on my cell phone app."

Luke nodded. "Let's go check them out."

Hannah hurried out with Luke to check the surveillance videos.

Caleb turned to Penny who had fear in her eyes as she clung to Missy. She had to be asking herself the same question he was: How had someone found them?

Had he been premature in telling Agent Sinclair that the leak couldn't possibly be from his office? But no one from his office had known they were leaving Missy here with Hannah. He hadn't even told Luke and he knew Hannah wouldn't have said anything to anyone.

None of this made sense to him. He wracked his brain for an answer.

He didn't have any yet—but he was determined to find them. Someone had followed them or tracked them here.

And Penny and Missy wouldn't be safe until he uncovered who.

# EIGHT

Penny was relieved when they finally arrived back at the cabin in the woods. It had begun to feel like a safe place for her. Caleb had been right that it was isolated enough to keep them hidden and he'd made certain, as they made the return drive, that no one was following them.

Missy jumped from the truck and ran into the trees to pick up a handful of leaves and toss them into the air. She laughed as they floated back down around her and Penny teared up at the sight. Her daughter rarely smiled and laughed these days, so it was good to see it now.

She glanced at Caleb who was also smiling at the scene. "Would it hurt anything to spend some time outside?" she asked.

He shook his head. "I think that's a great idea. It's a beautiful day and no one is going to come around out here." He knelt beside Missy. "Would you like to see the creek?"

She nodded and took his hand. Caleb turned to Penny. "You want to join us?" He held out his other hand to her and Penny took it.

It felt nice walking beside him as the warm spring afternoon air rolled over them. She soon heard the current of water from the creek Caleb had mentioned. It wasn't a small, shallow creek you could walk through, but a creek with what looked like a strong current. On the embankment was a canoe and a kayak, neither of which looked to have been used for a while. She figured if she tried to overturn either, something might scurry out from underneath, but she approached them anyway.

"Planning on taking a boat ride?" Caleb asked her.

"No, but it's good to know they're here in case we need to get away quickly. Without you, Missy and I are basically carless. These might come in handy if someone shows up."

"No one is going to find you here."

"It's better to be prepared and not need it than need it and not be prepared." She took a chance and overturned the canoe, surprised when nothing jumped—or slithered—out.

"Do you even know how to operate either of these?"

"Actually, I do. I spent summers as a teenager at my grandfather's lake house."

That seemed to be enough to convince Caleb that prepping these boats was a good idea. He pushed the kayak over, then helped her clean each of them up as best they could and made sure the paddles were close by as well.

Missy played and ran and jumped as they worked and Penny was glad for the time outside in the fresh air. They'd been holed up inside for too long but this isolated area provided the perfect excuse to allow her daughter some outside time. Caleb had made a good choice in bringing them here.

After clearing out the boats, she called for Missy to join them for another walk through the woods. Earlier, she had grimaced at each crunch of the leaves beneath their feet, but now she was relaxed enough to enjoy the walk and she didn't see anyone or even another cabin. They didn't walk far, but it felt good to stretch her legs, and having Caleb by her side gave her some added comfort. She was so thankful for him and all he'd done to keep her and Missy safe.

They'd walked for a while and after chatting about nature and the weather, he turned to something more serious. "I've been thinking about what you said earlier about being prepared in case something happens when I'm not around to protect you and Missy. Do you still have that gun you pointed at me the first night we met?"

Devon's gun. The one she'd pulled out when their vehicle was overturned and she'd thought the men chasing her were about to take them. "It's in my bag."

"Have you ever fired it?"

"No. It belonged to Missy's father. It stayed locked up in the back of the closet until this nightmare started. I took it because I thought I might need it."

"And you might." He stopped walking and turned to her. "I can't be with you both twenty-four hours a day and even if I could, at some point you'll enter witness protection and I won't see you again. I know the marshals will do their best to protect you, but you should also know how to protect yourself. I can teach you how to use that gun if you want."

She hesitated. She'd been so frightened that night and wasn't sure she could have held the men off even with the gun.

"If you don't want to, there's no pressure."

"No, I want to." She was surprised by how quickly she protested, then realized she really did want to learn. "I don't like feeling so helpless. You're right. You won't always be with us. I need to be able to protect Missy if something happens."

"We can set up some targets and you can get in some target practice. It won't bother anyone this far out. There aren't any neighbors for a long while."

He found some empty aluminum cans in his truck and set them up on a group of rocks by the creek while Penny went to retrieve the gun from her bag inside the cabin. It was heavy in her hand and intimidating, but she was just going to have to get used to it. She was glad Caleb had suggested teaching her. It was one more way she could defend herself and Missy.

She made certain Missy was preoccupied with playing in a clearing and let her know what they were doing before turning her attention to Caleb. He showed her how to load the gun, then walked her through several safety procedures. After he handed the weapon back to her, he showed her the proper way to stand and hold the gun to make her aim strong.

"Stand with your legs parted a few inches to anchor yourself in place." He waited until her feet were properly positioned before continuing. "Now, hold the gun with one hand and use the other to brace beneath it. That'll help you keep it straight because it's going to kick once you pull the trigger. And don't worry about wasting ammo. I have some in my truck that will fit this gun."

She nodded and tried to aim straight at the cans yet she couldn't stop her hands from shaking. Caleb stood behind her and, after a moment, he put his arms around her and used his hands to steady hers. "Hold it tight," he told her, showing her the proper method. However, his presence, while reassuring, was also distracting. She couldn't allow the feel of his arms against her or the scent of his cologne to distract her.

"You're ready," he told her, then backed away. "Fire when ready."

She aimed for the first can, then pulled the trigger. The force from the gun was strong and vibrated in her hand but she managed to keep her grip. She even hit the can. It went flying and a rush of excitement bubbled through her. She could do this. She glanced at Caleb who gave her the okay to fire again. She raised the gun and fired several more shots, hitting two out of the three remaining cans.

"I did it!" she exclaimed, turning to Caleb.

But another sound grabbed her attention once the ringing in her ears faded from the gun noise.

Missy screaming.

They both turned to her. She was shrieking at the top of her lungs. She was on the ground, her hands covering her ears and fear etched on her face.

Penny started toward her but Missy jumped up and ran toward the cabin. Panic shot through Penny at seeing her daughter so distressed. She handed Caleb the gun before running after her but he was quickly on her heels as she burst into the cabin and found Missy in a corner of the bedroom, her hands still covering her ears. Her lashes and cheeks were wet with tears.

"Missy, what is it? What's wrong?"

Of course, she couldn't say, but she didn't object when Penny pulled her into her arms. Instead, she clung to her mother even as the sobs continued.

Penny glanced up at Caleb, confusion spreading through her. She didn't understand. Nothing could have happened to Missy without them noticing since they'd been standing so close. Caleb seemed to have a knowing look on his face.

"I think the sound of gunfire might have reminded her of the shooting at the bank and at your hotel."

*Ugh!* She could kick herself for not seeing it. She hadn't even thought that might happen. Of course the sound of gunfire might bring back trauma. Her daughter had been in too many perilous situations involving guns.

Penny hugged her tightly. "It's okay, baby. It's okay. No one is going to hurt you. I was just shooting the gun to help protect us, okay?"

Missy nodded but didn't stop sobbing.

Caleb stepped out of the room and gave them some privacy. After a while, Missy calmed down and fell asleep. Penny moved her to the bed and let her rest, knowing that an emotional reaction like she'd had could wear anyone out.

She stepped into the living room and saw Caleb had his laptop and a mug. "I made coffee," he said. "Would you like some?"

"I'd love that. Thanks."

He set the laptop aside, then stood and walked to the kitchen area while Penny curled up on the couch.

"I'm sorry I frightened her," he said. "I wasn't thinking."

"Neither of us were. It didn't occur to me that the sound of gunfire might set her off like that. I should have realized."

He handed her the full cup. "How is she?"

"She's cried herself to sleep."

He sat beside her on the couch, then leaned over and picked up Missy's drawing pad and flipped through it. "No kid should have to see the things she has."

Penny set down the mug before she could drop it as a wave of guilt rushed through her. "She shouldn't have to deal with this. I should have been able to find a way out for us. Why does she have to keep reliving this? She needs therapy and we can't stay in one place long enough for me to even get her the help she needs. I'm failing her."

He pulled her into his arms. "You are not failing her. You're doing everything you can to keep her safe."

"It's not enough."

"It has to be." He locked eyes with her. "It has to be for now—but someday, this will end, Penny, and then you'll start the task of picking up your lives. She'll be able to get the help she needs. For now, her physical safety has to take priority."

She leaned into his embrace and let his logical words soothe her open wounds. He was right, of course. They were doing what they had to do. But knowing that was true didn't make her feel much better when she had to hold and rock her crying, hysterical daughter to sleep.

She couldn't even say how she was keeping it all together when crying hysterically was all she wanted to do too.

She placed her head on his chest and listened to the sound of his heart. It was calming. She couldn't remember the last time she'd felt so protected by anyone in her life, even her own late husband.

She closed her eyes and listened to the sound of his heart beating and the chirp of the crickets until they lulled her to sleep.

The emotional toll this was having on both Penny and Missy wrecked Caleb. He was used to walking into dangerous situations, but seeing both these females so emotionally devastated was more than he could stand. He preferred a gun in his hand to a box of tissues, but holding Penny and sharing her pain had reaffirmed something inside him about his duty to protect them—not just physically but emotionally too.

They'd both napped for the rest of the afternoon, then he'd made them a light supper of soup and grilled cheese before they'd turned in for the night.

Once they were asleep, he phoned his cousin to check in and see if Agent Sinclair had updated him on anything new.

"She's pulled financial records and background checks on everyone in her office and yours but, so far, all she'll say is that she's confidant the leak isn't coming from her office."

It had barely been one day so Caleb knew she hadn't had enough time to go through all those records. He was also certain no one in his office was responsible for giving up the location for Penny and Missy's meeting with Marshal Dryer—if for no other reason than because no one in his office had known.

"Have there been any updates on the bombing?"

"Nothing. I spoke with Marshal Kirk. Marissa made certain to hide her location on her GPS and avoid any cameras while en route to the diner so that's making it harder to determine if she was followed. However, Marshal Kirk doesn't believe she was. He was adamant that she was good at her job and would have been able to spot a tail. I believe him. She was always very security conscious. She knew her charges' lives depended on it."

"So that only leaves the bomber learning the location before the meet-up. The question is how."

"We're still working on that. This group must have some deep connections to be able to gain this kind of information. It's scary."

Caleb was thinking the same thing and it didn't bode well for Penny and Missy.

"What about Hannah? Have you spoken to her?"

"I did. She's still shaken up. She thinks she let you down by allowing someone inside the house."

He hated to hear that. She'd done what she had to do in order to protect Missy and he couldn't have asked for anything more. He would call her and reassure her about that. She had no reason to blame herself. Besides, he'd been the one to place her in that situation in the first place.

"I also questioned Joiner once he regained consciousness."

Caleb was glad to hear that his officer had come around. He should have reached out himself to make certain Joiner was okay, but he'd been so focused on Penny and Missy that he hadn't thought of it. He was glad to see his cousin had stepped up in his place. "How is he?"

"He suffered a concussion but he'll recover. Unfortunately, he can't identify the man he saw sneaking around the house, and the cameras were no help in identifying him either."

"Did Joiner say if he told anyone he was guarding Missy or where he was?"

"He claims he didn't tell anyone."

Caleb pinched the bridge of his nose, feeling a headache forming. "How did the assailants know that Missy would be there? I don't understand it."

"Neither do I. We must be missing something. I'll keep on working on it. In the meantime, you focus on keeping them safe."

Caleb ended the call but wondered if he was doing the right thing. He wanted to be a part of that investigation, certain he could find the answers, but that was just ego. Luke was extremely capable and Caleb trusted him completely. If he had to trust anyone else to figure it out, it was Luke.

He settled on the couch and tried to clear his mind. He had a job and that was keeping Penny and Missy safe. He took that duty seriously. He couldn't fully explain his desire to help these two or how he'd become so invested. His admiration for Penny was morphing into something he couldn't quite put his finger on. He liked spending time with them and he worried about Missy's ability to heal from the trauma she'd suffered.

He wasn't sure how long he'd been asleep when a noise outside grabbed his attention. He was used to hearing the rustle of animals and chirps of the birds, but this was something different. This noise had him reaching for his gun.

Outside the curtain, dawn's light peeked through, but as he moved closer to the window, he spotted a figure moving outside.

He didn't know how but they'd been found.

He glanced at the closed bedroom door where Penny and Missy were still sleeping. He had to get to them out of here and moved to somewhere safe.

It was time for them to leave. The fishing cabin had been compromised.

Penny was shaken awake by strong hands on her shoulder. It took her a moment to pull herself from a deep sleep, but the urgency in Caleb's voice alarmed her.

"Penny, wake up. We have to go."

She rubbed her eyes to clear away the sleep. "Wh-what's the matter?"

"Someone is outside."

With that, clearing away the cobwebs in her mind wasn't a problem anymore. Adrenaline shot through her. She pushed back the blanket, then roused Missy and slipped her shoes on as Missy did the same. Caleb had his gun in his hand—another indication of how serious this matter was. Fear raced through her. They should have been safe here.

She dug through her bag and found Devon's gun again where she'd returned it to after the incident with Missy. She'd hoped not to have to use it but was glad Caleb showed her how, just in case. She pulled the bag over her shoulder, then took Missy's hand while Caleb went to check the front window.

He came back and the grim look on his face told her they were in trouble.

"What is it?"

"We need to go out the back way now."

"Shouldn't we stay inside?" It seemed more logical to her to lock the doors and hide but he shook his head.

"If they trap us in the cabin, we're in serious trouble. They could bust their way in and we would be trapped. Or they could set fire to the cabin to smoke us out."

She held up her hand to end his explanation. "I get it. We have to get out now."

"Before they surround us."

He didn't say it but the crease of his brow gave away what he'd left unspoken—*unless they already have.*

He urged them to the back door, then motioned for them to wait while he exited first. He raised his gun and stepped outside, scanning the area for intruders. When none appeared, he waved them out.

Penny breathed a sigh of relief that at least they weren't trapped. She grabbed her daughter's hand and pulled her outside.

"Head toward the tree line," Caleb said, his voice low so as not to alert the intruders.

She darted toward the tree line. Caleb was right behind them, urging them along. A chill ran down her spine that matched the cool of the morning. At least it was daylight and they weren't running in complete darkness. Then again, perhaps that would have hidden them better. Her mind raced with anxiety but an underlying question ran through her. How had they been found again?

Caleb stopped them and pulled them down to crouch against a tree. His entire body was tense and on high alert. He pulled his cell phone from his pocket and hit a button, then spoke when the caller on the other end answered.

"Luke, it's Caleb. I'm at grandpa's old fishing cabin with Penny and Missy. Someone's here. They found us."

She heard Luke's voice on the other end but couldn't make out what he was saying. Caleb nodded, then ended the call and slipped the phone back into his pocket.

"We have to get out of here but we can't go back to the truck. The man I saw was at the front of the house. I didn't see anyone else but I have to assume he's not alone."

"What do we do?"

"There's another cabin about a mile away through the woods. Luke can meet us there."

She nodded. At least it was a plan. She clutched Missy to her, thankful Caleb had been here when the intruder arrived.

Suddenly, shots rang out, hitting the tree they were crouching beside. Penny fell backward into the wet grass as Caleb returned fire, the sound causing Missy to scream and jerk from her arms. She took off running and Penny scrambled to her feet and ran after her as more shots fired.

"Missy!" She was inches away from grabbing her daughter's arm when Missy turned to her, the abrupt motion causing her daughter to slip on the mud. Her feet went out from under her and she slid down the embankment, screaming as she rolled toward the creek. Penny dove for her and grabbed her, pulling her up before she splashed into the water below.

Only, climbing back up the embankment proved difficult. The current threatened them on one side and the muddy embankment on the other. She heaved Missy onto her hip as the girl clung to her neck and she fumbled to get her footing on the embankment as shots rang out above them.

They had to get back up before they slid into the water.

Suddenly, Caleb appeared and took hold of her, pulling them both up onto the grass with what seemed like effortless ease.

"Were either of you hit?"

She shook her head, then checked Missy. "No. We're fine. He didn't hit us." But they were caked in mud and freezing.

He pulled them back toward a large tree for cover. "I only heard shots coming from one direction. The shooter might be alone after all. If I can sneak back around the cabin and catch him from behind, I can stop him."

"How can you be sure he's alone? There might be someone else hiding out."

He shook his head. "If there were, I would have seen or heard them when he started firing at us. This is our chance to capture him and get answers about how they found us. We have to take the risk."

She clutched Missy to her. "What should we do?"

"Stay here and stay hidden." He pressed the cell phone into her hand. "Luke's cell phone is number two on my speed dial. Call him if this goes sideways, then head into the woods along that trail to the Westbrooks' cabin. Don't stop until you get there."

She hugged Missy to her and they crouched down by a tree, ignoring the wetness of the grass and morning dew. Neither were wearing a jacket and the chill of the morning and the mud bit against her skin. Missy was shivering but Penny couldn't be certain if it was because of the weather and mud on them or because of the danger they were facing.

She watched as Caleb darted behind a tree, then disappeared. She hardly even heard his footsteps over her heart, which was hammering so loudly she was certain the attacker could hear it.

She dug through her bag for Devon's gun and pulled it out. "Lord, please keep us safe." She whispered the prayer without even thinking. She'd surprised herself, but if God was in a generous mood, then perhaps He would help them this time.

She needed Him to come through for them now.

She swept her gaze through the woods but saw nothing. Every crunch and rustle of leaves had her gripping the gun tighter. She felt exposed outside but Caleb had told them to stay put. She crouched behind a tree and strained to listen, hearing nothing but the sounds of nature and Missy whimpering beside her. Suddenly, the crunch of sticks caused her to spin around. A man stood over her. She raised the gun at him but he knocked it out of her hand before she could fire. He shoved her to the ground, then grabbed Missy and pulled her to him.

"No," Penny screamed as he turned to run with her daughter in his arms. "Caleb, help!"

She scrambled to her feet and grabbed Missy's foot as Missy squirmed to get free from his grip. Penny wasn't going to let this man take her daughter.

He spun around and smacked her, sending Penny to the ground. Her breath left her and the branches scraped her hands as she fell, but she couldn't let that stop her. Missy's life depended on it.

She grabbed his ankle and tripped him. He fell and Missy escaped from his grasp and took off running. Penny felt a moment of pure relief, but it gave way to pain when her assailant kicked Penny in the face. She fell backward as pain radiated through her cheek. She jumped to her feet and ran to Missy, pulling her daughter into her arms.

The attacker picked up a branch and swung it at them, causing Penny to stumble. She rolled down the embankment with Missy still held tight. They both hit the water with a splash. The cold water was like a thousand knives stabbing her. Her breath caught and she tried reaching for something to anchor them but the current was pulling her under. Missy's hand slipped from hers and Penny frantically tried to grab her but the current separated them and Penny couldn't reach her.

She heard gunshots and tried to scream for Missy but the water pulled her under again and she couldn't breathe.

Panic filled her. She was drowning and her daughter was too.

They were going to die in this water.

Strong hands grabbed her and pulled her up out of the water. She started to fight but went limp when she realized it was Caleb lifting her in his arms and pulling her to the edge of the creek. Once she was out of the water, he went back in after Missy.

She fell onto the cold grass, struggling to catch her breath, as Caleb returned carrying Missy in his arms.

Penny ran to her. The little girl was soaking wet and barely breathing. Caleb listened to her, then performed CPR until she coughed and spat out water from her lungs as Penny stood shivering helplessly.

The little girl whimpered and Penny fell onto the grass, relief flooding her at the sound of her daughter's cries.

"We need to get out of here but, first, we need to get her dry so Missy doesn't get sick," Caleb stated, and she agreed. He scooped Missy up and ran back toward the cabin.

Penny grabbed his arm. "Wait, what about the man who attacked us?"

"He's long gone," Caleb assured her. "I wounded him, and he took off running. I heard a vehicle roaring away before I jumped into the water after you and Missy. He's gone."

He carried the girl into the cabin and placed her on

the ground in front of the fireplace. "I'll get some more wood for the fire. You get a blanket and a set of dry clothes. We need to get you both warmed up quickly."

He vanished out the door and Penny hurried for a blanket and a change of clothes for them both. She quickly dried Missy off, slipped a clean, dry nightgown over her head, then wrapped her in the blanket as Caleb reappeared and got the fire roaring again. Penny dried off and changed in the bedroom. By the time she returned, Missy's skin had returned to its natural color and the blueness around her lips had faded.

Caleb returned with a clean pair of clothes. "I had an extra set in the closet from the last time I was here, but my boots are soaked. How's she doing?"

"She seems to be better. She's sleeping."

"She needs rest and time to recover. Unfortunately, we don't have time. That guy we saw might have been here alone but that doesn't mean he's working alone. Now that he knows our location, he or his friends will surely be coming back to finish what they started. We don't have a lot of time. We should get out of here as soon as we can."

She stroked Missy's hair. They'd dodged the would-be assassin and survived a trip into the creek, but what would they do now? "Where can we go?"

"I called Luke while I was out by the truck. I'm taking you both back to my family's ranch. It's the safest place for you both right now until we figure something else out."

"Won't that put your family in danger?"

"We know how to protect ourselves. Luke will be

around to help guard the place. It's the best play we have right now. We'll figure out our next move once I know you and Missy are safe."

She nodded. She knew they couldn't remain here. The cabin had been breached and it was no longer safe.

After he'd changed, he picked up Missy and loaded her into the truck while Penny gathered their few belongings. They were on the road again before she knew it. Missy was restless but had trouble staying awake.

"Do you think she needs to go to the hospital?"

"She wasn't in the water long," Caleb said. "I think she just needs time to recover from the morning's ordeal, but it's your call. Whatever you want to do, I'll do my best to make sure you're both safe. You should know though, that going to the hospital would be dangerous. The FBI could show up and detain you or the bad guys could find you."

In the end, she decided against the hospital. Missy seemed to be better. "I just want to get her somewhere safe."

Would they be safe at Caleb's ranch? She could only hope so. She didn't like the idea of putting other people in danger, but she trusted Caleb and she knew that they needed a new place to hide.

When would this nightmare finally be over?

For now, they were safe—but who knew how long that safety would last?

# NINE

Missy fell back asleep as they headed into town. An hour later, Caleb turned off the main road and under a sign that read Harmon Ranch. As they drove down the dirt road, Penny spotted green pastureland with horses grazing in the fields, split rail fences, stables and a large red barn.

He drove past them all to a massive house where he parked. She was awed by the size of it. Her entire apartment building where they'd lived could have fit inside. "You live here?"

"Yes, along with Luke and his family. It belonged to my grandfather but he left it to me and my three cousins when he died earlier this year. There's plenty of room so that we're not all tripping all over one another."

"Are you sure we won't be inconveniencing anyone by staying here?"

"Not at all. Besides, I'm sure Hannah will be glad to see you both again. Luke said she was really worried that she let you down."

Penny would be glad for the chance to see her again too. She'd been so freaked out about the break-in that she'd never gotten the opportunity to properly thank Hannah for protecting her daughter. But that brought them right back to the fact that now that they were staying at the ranch, they were putting even more people in danger.

Caleb must have seen her hesitation because he reached for her hand and gave it a squeeze. "Don't worry so much. I promised to keep you safe—and everyone else here will too. Together, we will figure a way out of this."

She wasn't so sure. She'd felt safe at the cabin yet they'd still been discovered there. How difficult would it be for the bad guys to find them here? With Luke here for extra protection, that should have made her feel better but it didn't. She wouldn't ever truly relax until she knew for certain that her daughter was out of danger.

She woke Missy and they headed inside. Hannah hurried out to greet them, pulling them both into a hug that nearly caused Penny to tear up. Her genuine warmth was refreshing.

"I'm so happy to see you both again. Are you hurt? I heard they found you at the cabin. I was shocked when Luke told me about it. Honestly, I had forgotten that place even existed."

"That was kind of the point," Caleb agreed. "It should have been safe. I don't know yet how we were found."

"Well, you're here now and you will definitely be safe here. Caleb and Luke will make sure of it, plus I'll be here too. I won't allow anything to happen to you."

"But you don't live here," Penny protested. "I don't want to take you away from your home."

"I have a room here too. I moved away from the ranch when I got married but since my husband passed away, I often stay here during the week or on special occasions. This is one of those special occasions. I won't leave until you're both safe."

She was grateful for Hannah's determination. Penny actually felt better having her around. Plus, the way Missy hugged her touched Penny's heart. Hannah was the only other person besides Caleb that Missy seemed to be opening up to. Perhaps her daughter was finally beginning to heal from all she'd been through.

Wishful thinking, of course. They hadn't been in one place long enough for her to heal.

But, if they could prevent any further trauma to her, maybe she could fully recover and become the happy little girl she'd been before this nightmare started.

Oh, how Penny wanted to see her that way again.

"Let's get you both settled in," Hannah said.

Penny took Missy's hand and followed Hannah up the staircase and down a long hallway with Caleb behind them. Hannah pushed open a door that led into a spacious room with a queen-size bed and an attached bathroom. "Here you go. I assumed you'd want to share a room."

"Yes, this is perfect." It was actually more room than they'd ever had.

Caleb carried their bags and set them on the bed. He touched her arm and Penny turned to look up at him. "I don't want to leave you but I'd like to go find Luke and check in with him. Will you two be okay here for a while?"

The last thing she wanted was for him to leave but

they all needed answers. "We'll be fine," Penny assured him, despite her hesitation.

"They will be," Hannah insisted. "I'll make you both some breakfast." She knelt by Missy. "Would you like some pancakes and syrup?"

Missy smiled and nodded, causing Penny's heart to leap with joy. It was good to see her smile.

"That sounds delicious, Hannah. Thank you."

Caleb leaned in and gave Hannah a kiss on the cheek. "Thank you for looking out for them," he told her, then turned back to Penny. "I'll check in on you soon."

They watched him leave, then Hannah reached out and touched her arm. "I've never seen Caleb so determined. I'm glad he brought you here."

"Me too," Penny admitted. She'd loved the isolation of the cabin but being welcomed into this home with open arms and reassurances warmed her heart. She only hoped it was the right decision.

"After the morning you've had, you probably want to rest. I'll bring breakfast to you, then y'all can come downstairs whenever you're ready."

Hannah walked out, closing the door behind her. Penny took a deep breath. They were here now and hopefully they would be safe.

She turned to Missy. "Let's clean up. Then we'll eat."

Their abrupt awakening this morning, then fighting for their lives, had indeed left her worn out. She couldn't wait to get something to eat and fall back into bed.

Caleb hated to leave the ranch now that Penny and Missy were there, but he needed to check in with his office and get an update from Luke about the investigation.

He wasn't worried about their safety. He knew Hannah would make certain they were safe and he'd alerted Ed, the ranch manager, and the ranch hands to watch out for strangers on the property. They would be fine until he returned. He wouldn't leave if he didn't believe that.

He parked in the back lot and entered the police station through the back office, nearly running into Abby, Luke's wife, as she exited.

"Abby, it's good to see you."

"You too, Caleb." She held up a cooler bag. "I brought Luke some lunch. He's been working on this case so hard that we haven't had much time together. I thought it would be nice to take a break and spend a half hour with one another."

Caleb's face warmed. He was monopolizing Luke but he couldn't be sorry. "I'm thankful for all his help."

"And I know he's glad to do it. Honestly, I think he's beginning to miss his FBI life. Life with a wife and two kids isn't exactly glamorous."

"That's ridiculous. He's crazy about you and those kids."

She pushed a strand of hair from her face and he saw how forlorn she truly looked. "I can tell that he misses the thrill of working a case."

"Yes, well, sometimes that thrill isn't all it's cracked up to be."

"Did he tell you that Brett had offered him a job?"

Caleb was floored by that news. "He didn't." If Luke had kept Brett's job offer at his security firm a secret from Caleb, it was because he hadn't dismissed the idea completely. Maybe Abby had a right to wonder if her husband was feeling restless in small-town Jessup.

"Don't mind me, Caleb. I shouldn't be talking to you about this. I know how close you and Luke are and I wouldn't want to get in the way of any confidences you two share. I'm going to go. I'm due back at the TV station in a few minutes."

She started toward her car but Caleb stopped her. "Did Luke mention that I was bringing Penny and Missy to the ranch? They're there now."

She nodded. "Yes, he told me. The kids are both sleeping over at a friend's house tonight and I'm filling in for the nighttime anchor for the next week so we might not be around much."

He didn't tell her that might be a good thing for their own safety. Abby was as sharp as they came—she'd no doubt figured that out already.

"I'll try to stop by and say hello though." She climbed into her car, then waved to him as she drove off.

Luke was in the conference room, already back at work even as he finished a sandwich which she'd obviously brought for him.

"I just saw your wife leaving," Caleb told him as he walked in.

Luke turned to him. "She brought food for you too," he said, pointing to another small cooler bag in the corner.

"Thanks. She also told me about the job offer from Brett."

That got a response from him. He dropped his sandwich, then leaned back in his chair. "I was going to tell you."

"You're thinking about it?"

"I haven't ruled it out. The offer is appealing."

"I thought you were happy in Jessup. You and Abby seem pretty happy to me."

"And we are, Caleb. That's not what this is about." He shrugged as he struggled to find words to explain. "I'm not a rancher," he finally said. "Ed runs the ranch. You're the police. Abby reports the news. I love my life here. I love my wife and my daughter, and Dustin is like a son to me. I guess I am a little restless. Aside from helping you with this case and helping Brett and Jaycee, I don't have that much to do."

Jaycee, Brett's wife, had been targeted by a killer several months ago. Brett had brought her to the ranch in order to keep her safe from her attacker, though they'd decided not to stay in Jessup.

It wasn't the right fit for Brett, but up until this minute, Caleb believed that it had been for Luke. Remaining in Jessup, marrying his high school sweetheart, getting to know the daughter he hadn't realized he'd had. Living at Harmon Ranch had been natural for them, especially after Abby's childhood home had burned to the ground. At first, Caleb had wondered how it would work with them all living there, but he'd come to love the company. He hadn't realized before how empty the big house had been and, with this possible news, he didn't relish how empty it might be again.

Harmon Ranch needed a family to make it a home

and that's what Luke and Abby had done. Would Caleb still see it as such without them?

His mind went to Missy running through the woods and playing with the leaves. She might love the open fields and the horses and even the old hideout where he and his cousins had played as kids. He could imagine making a home there with her and Penny. He quickly pushed those thoughts away. It was futile to even imagine such things. Penny and Missy would be leaving once it was safe for them to do so. Harmon Ranch could never be their home.

Besides, he'd decided a long time ago that a family wasn't in his future, back when he'd yet to meet a woman he cared to build a family with.

Until now.

He pushed those thoughts away.

Even if Penny Jackson was the kind of woman he could imagine a future with, it wasn't to be. The best outcome for Penny and Missy was that they would enter witness protection and he would never see them again.

He'd never meant to get his heart involved, but somehow Penny Jackson and her sweet, troubled daughter had squirmed their way past his barriers. Now, he was doomed to get his heart broken. But he couldn't deny his feelings for her any longer. He'd known it the moment he'd realized she'd fallen into the creek. This was no longer about keeping a mother and child safe out of a sense of duty or respect for her sacrifice. He was worried about their safety because he cared about them personally—and that was going to get his heart shattered.

There was no good way out of this mess he'd made. She couldn't stay here. Witness protection was her best chance at building a normal life for herself and Missy. He would have no choice but to eventually be separated from them and he wasn't sure his heart could stand it.

But he also couldn't allow that little girl to be harmed.

He steered the conversation back to the threat against them. "The good news is that Penny and Missy are back at the ranch—safe under Hannah's supervision. Ed is having the ranch hands set up a perimeter and I'm sending a couple of officers to stand guard. The bad news is that we still have no idea who's after them or how they keep getting found. The man who attacked us at the fishing cabin was small and thin. He came alone but he was still nearly able to grab Missy."

"Can you at least identify him?"

"I didn't recognize him from the mug shots I've seen of the bank robbers, but I'll try to put together a sketch and look through some photographs to see if I can identify him as one of their associates. I shot him though so we should put out an alert to local ERs in case he came in."

He should have done that earlier but he'd been more concerned with getting Penny and Missy safely to the ranch. If this guy had showed up at any of the nearby hospitals for medical attention, he was likely long gone by now.

Luke made the call, then turned back to him. "Do we need to take a crime scene crew up to the fishing cabin?"

"I don't think they'll find anything of use but it might

not hurt. If they can find some blood, it might help to connect him to the attack." Hopefully they might also find some indication of how he'd found them there. "I know we weren't followed to the cabin. I just don't understand how he found us."

"The fact that he was alone might indicate that he wasn't expecting to find you either. Maybe he learned about the cabin and took a chance on checking it out."

"Maybe, but how many people knew that place was even there? It seems like a stretch that he could have found out about it at all."

Luke agreed. "I'd certainly forgotten about it."

Caleb leaned against the table. "Have you heard anything from Agent Sinclair?" He hoped something had been discovered.

Luke pulled up a surveillance video. "Not much. Her team managed to locate surveillance video on our four bank robbers once they were released. All four of them are still in Kentucky. They haven't left the state."

"That's good news. They're not in town."

"And it doesn't look like they're planning to come this way. That tells me they believe the matter is being handled."

Caleb agreed with Luke's assessment. If they weren't doing whatever they could to ensure they didn't wind up back in prison, then they must already be pretty confident that someone capable was handling it for them. It wasn't like career criminals, violent ones at that, to sit back and do nothing. "Is Agent Sinclair any closer to finding information on their accomplices? Anyone who might be handling this matter for them?"

"Not yet. She has agents going through their known associates but, so far, they're all accounted for."

Caleb sighed and rubbed his chin as he watched surveillance video of the four bank robbers going about their lives while a little girl and her mother cowered in fear. His blood boiled. "Then we're missing someone. We know there are at least two men in town trying to hurt Penny and Missy. They have to be working for one or all of these men."

"Agreed." Luke pulled up another surveillance image. "So I contacted several businesses in town and convinced them to share their security footage. This is an image we received from a camera in downtown Jessup."

The video showed a man in a black pickup parked at the curb in front of the coffee shop.

The image on the screen wasn't clear enough to make an identification, but Caleb had to agree it matched roughly the body type of one of the men he'd encountered that night when her car had been run off the road. All he could say for certain was that this definitely wasn't the man he'd fought at the cabin. That attacker had been thinner and wirier than this guy. "What about the men from the bus station? Have there been any hits on facial recognition?"

"Again, the images from the bus station aren't helpful. None got a clear image of their faces and facial recognition hasn't been able to match them."

Another dead end. Even with FBI resources, these men were remaining under the radar. "How is this possible?"

"They're experienced at laying low."

"They have to be on someone's radar somewhere.

Where are they staying? Where are they eating? What are they doing all day—when they aren't terrorizing Penny? And what about their reasons for taking the job—are they closely tied to the robbers or are they just thugs for hire? Have we tried checking the financial records of the bank robbers? Maybe they paid these men for the job."

"Agent Sinclair's team can't find any record of money transfers but they're also still poring through those files. It's a lot and I'm sure they have money that can't be accounted for. It's doubtful they deposited the money they got from robbing banks into any kind of officially regulated and monitored bank account. And, if they're using cash and have someone acting on their behalf, it'll be much harder to uncover those transactions."

Caleb sighed as he fell into a chair. This was not the news he wanted to hear. They were no closer to finding a way out of this mess. Men were in town to kill Penny and Missy and they were not able to find them or even identify who they were. It seemed hopeless.

Thankfully, he didn't put his hope in the things of this world. God knew the identity of these men and where they were. He knew a way out of this. It was up to Caleb, Luke, and the other officers to seek His guidance to figure a way out.

"And what about the leaks? Any news on that?"

"Nothing new. No one wants to admit there might be leaks in their agency."

Caleb pulled a frustrated hand through his hair. They weren't making any progress and it might be because of the FBI and Marshals' refusal to take a hard look at their own agencies.

"I was able to get a list of everyone who had knowledge of this case from the people in the US Attorney's office to the FBI and Marshals. Agent Sinclair sent it over."

He pulled it up on the screen and Caleb went down the names. They meant nothing to him but perhaps Penny remembered some of them. "Can you send this to my phone? I want to run these names by Penny."

"It's doubtful she knows most of them. There are a lot of people involved in investigations that victims and witnesses never meet."

"I know but I'm grasping at straws."

Luke nodded, understanding. He copied the file and e-mailed it to Caleb, whose phone dinged with the notification. Still looking at the computer, he focused in on a particular name. "Who is this Dr. Anna Williams?"

Luke dug through the records. "Looks like she's a child psychologist who was hired by the AG's office."

"Penny didn't mention that Missy saw a child psychologist."

"Maybe she never had the opportunity to see her before Penny took Missy and ran. It's possible she merely reviewed the file." He dug deeper into the files Agent Sinclair had sent him. "Here it is. It looks like she did see her right after the bank robbery. She's on the witness list as an expert they were planning to call to prove that Missy can be an effective witness. The defense argued that Missy's testimony is suspect given her age."

"They don't think she's old enough to be a witness?"

"That's what the defense was arguing but the matter never went before the judge because Penny and Missy disappeared. Without her presence, the judge wasn't able to question her so he couldn't make a ruling. That was when the case started to fall apart—ending in the release of the suspects for lack of evidence."

It didn't seem fair. These men had been released only because they'd sent someone to kill Missy. It was obvious witness tampering but they needed to find the evidence in order to prove it.

Bank robbery, witness tampering, plus murder. These were dangerous men after Penny and her daughter. And so far, the people who were supposed to protect them hadn't done nearly enough.

But they *had* brought in a psychologist to talk to Missy. Caleb was surprised that Penny hadn't mentioned that, especially since he knew that she was worried about getting help for her daughter.

"I'll make sure she looks over this list. Someone might have stood out as acting odd to her."

Luke sighed. "It's unlikely but it can't hurt."

"Thank you, Luke, for everything you've done. I mean it. Without your intervention, dealing with Agent Sinclair would have been more difficult. I'm glad you've got my back."

"Always. I can see how important Penny and Missy are to you."

His face warmed. Were his feelings for them so obvious? He had to do better at concealing them.

He nodded. "They're counting on me to make sure they're safe, but I'm not sure how to do that."

"You like her and you won't even let yourself admit it."

"What difference does it make? Assuming I can protect her until I can hand them over to the Marshals, they'll still be leaving. She'll be leaving. What's the point of getting caught up in my feelings?"

Luke shook his head. "I've seen you run into a firefight without hesitating for a second. I once even watched you jump into the lake to rescue a dog from an alligator, but you won't admit that you're falling for Penny. What are you so afraid of?"

He stared at Luke for a moment. Was that what he was? Afraid? Maybe so. Getting a physical injury didn't scare him one bit. Placing himself in harm's way barely warranted a second thought. But putting his heart out there and having it shattered… He wasn't sure he could take that again.

He thought about that first day he'd seen her at Walker's Grocery. He'd immediately been struck by her beauty, but there were plenty of beautiful women in Jessup. It wasn't until she and Missy had nearly been killed that she'd piqued his interest. "It was the way she clung to Missy."

"What was?"

"The first day I saw them, Penny was clinging to her. I saw her fight or flight responses kicking in and I knew something was wrong. I could tell that she was running from something. I didn't know what, but the fact that she was holding so tightly to that little girl just struck me. I knew at that moment that, whatever trouble they were in, she would do anything to protect her child."

"Oh." Luke nodded and seemed to understand.

His cousin knew his history, so no more explanation was needed. "I admire Penny for sacrificing so much to keep her daughter safe. I haven't known too many women who would do that, you know."

"I know and it's okay. I admire her too. It's obvious she would do anything for her daughter. But, Caleb, don't be so quick to put up your defenses. Would it be such a terrible thing to admit you like this woman?"

"If I do my job correctly, then she'll be leaving. What's the point of acting on any feelings I might have for her?"

"You know, I wondered that myself when Abby and I first reconnected. I had no idea what the future held but I was so sure we wouldn't be able to be together so I held myself in check. I tried my best not to fall back in love with her. Now, I'm so grateful I didn't lose her."

"But I *will* lose Penny, Luke. That's the point of all this. She's going away. She'll enter witness protection and I'll never see her again. I know what the future holds and every future I can imagine ends with us going our separate ways."

"Maybe you're right, but, Caleb, I've never seen you this way. This woman and her daughter have opened up something inside you—something that I always knew was there. Something that I don't think you should ignore. Maybe just enjoy it while you can." After speaking his piece, Luke walked away, leaving Caleb to his thoughts.

He spent the next hour dealing with paperwork. He signed off on the most important issues then prioritized the ones that could wait and passed the rest off to his deputy chief to handle. He continued thinking about his cousin's words as he drove back to the ranch.

Luke was right that he should enjoy the time spent with Penny and Missy while they had it. He had to face the truth that he was going to be devastated when they left no matter what. It was too late to guard his heart. They'd already become important to him.

Their futures were intertwined in his—even if they spent those futures apart.

# TEN

Penny awoke with a start, at first unaware of her surroundings. But within a few moments, the memory of coming to Harmon Ranch fell into place. She reached for her daughter and fear rustled through her when she realized the spot beside her on the bed was empty. Missy had been napping next to her when she'd fallen asleep. Now, she was gone.

Penny jumped up and hurried into the adjoining bathroom. She wasn't there either.

Panic filled her. She dug for the cell phone Caleb had given her, hoping she had a message from him stating he'd come and got Missy while she was sleeping, but there were no messages.

She hit the speed dial to call him, doing her best to tamp down the fear that was rising in her throat.

"I can't find Missy," she exclaimed when he answered.

His voice was calm when he responded but she heard the hint of panic beneath it. "Where are you?"

"In the bedroom at the ranch. We were taking a nap together, but I woke up and she was gone."

"It's okay. Maybe she just went downstairs and went exploring."

"No, she wouldn't have gone exploring without me." Maybe once upon a time before the bank robbery she might have, but not now.

"I'm just up the road on my way back to the ranch. We'll find her."

She ended the call, then rushed from the bedroom, opening every door she came across and searching for her daughter and calling her name. There was no sign of her.

She rushed down the staircase and heard humming coming from the kitchen. She ran toward the sound and found Hannah using the mixer and Missy, an apron draped over her, standing on a chair, helping Hannah.

"Missy!" Penny ran to her and scooped her up in her arms.

"Oh, I'm sorry," Hannah said when she saw how distressed Penny was. "I came upstairs to check on you and Missy was awake, so I invited her to come lend me a hand. She's helping me bake cookies for my church's bake sale."

Relief flooded Penny. Missy was still inside the house. She was safe. She knew she'd overreacted but she couldn't stop the fear that had swept through her. She tried to steady her racing heart as Missy squirmed in her grasp as if nothing had happened. "No, I'm sorry, Hannah. I woke up and panicked. I should have known she wouldn't run off. I just can't believe I didn't hear you come into the bedroom." Of course Missy would go with Hannah. Missy felt safe with her—and that was a good thing. It meant she got to have experiences like this. Baking cookies seemed like such a normal thing for a little girl to want to do.

The back door slammed and Caleb came stomping into the kitchen, jerking to a stop when he spotted her holding Missy. His face held panic at first before his expression morphed into relief. "You found her."

"It's okay," she told him, feeling her face flush with embarrassment for her overreaction. "She was with Hannah. They were baking cookies."

Caleb's entire body relaxed. He walked over and put his arms around them both, leaning his head against hers. "That's a relief. You had me worried." He tickled Missy's chin and she giggled before successfully escaping Penny's arms. She climbed back onto the chair to continue helping Hannah.

Caleb sighed. "No one can resist Hannah's baking."

She turned to him. "I'm sorry I overreacted."

He waved away her apology. "I understand why you did. I knew no one could get in here without someone knowing, but after all that's happened I was worried too. I shouldn't have left."

"Did you at least find out anything?"

He started to speak, then stopped. "Why don't we take a walk?"

She glanced at Hannah and Missy, rolling chunks of cookie dough and placing them on a baking sheet. He must have sensed her apprehension at leaving her.

"She'll be fine," he whispered. "And we won't go far."

Finally, she acquiesced and followed him through the kitchen and outside.

"Let's take a walk down by the stables."

Now she was growing nervous. What could he have uncovered that would necessitate not speaking in front of Missy and Hannah? "Did you find out something?"

"No, I just thought it would be nice to give you some breathing room and stretch your legs a bit. Missy is enjoying herself with Hannah."

"I know. I'm hovering."

"You have good reason to but it's not necessary at the moment."

He was right about that—and he was also right about the pleasures of having a moment for herself. It felt good to be able to take a breath and not have to worry every moment. Plus, it was a beautiful day. She stopped and took a deep breath.

"Feel better?"

She opened her eyes and stared into his, getting lost in them. Her stomach fluttered at his smile and this time, it wasn't panic that stole her breath. "Much," she managed to say.

She shook her head to push away those thoughts. She was so grateful to Caleb for all he'd done for them and all he was still doing, and she couldn't deny her attraction to him, but falling for him was a mistake she couldn't afford to make. She had to keep herself focused. There was too much of a risk that something else terrible would happen while she was preoccupied. She had to put Missy's safety before anything—even her own happiness.

"So what did you and your cousin find?"

He pulled out his phone. "He sent me a list of all the

people involved in your case. I was hoping you could look at it and tell me who you recognize and if anything stood out to you about them."

She took the phone but wasn't sure she'd have anything useful to share. She doubted she could recall all the people she'd met since that day at the bank. They'd been questioned and shuffled around so many times and there had been a flurry of agents rushing around. "I'll do my best."

She scrolled through the list but didn't recognize most of the names. "I know Agent Sinclair, of course, and these two agents. I believe they were our escorts when we had to go somewhere."

"What about Dr. Anna Williams? Did Missy see her?"

She scrolled down until she found Dr. Williams's name. "Oh, yeah. She consulted with Missy about what she'd seen. I believe she was supposed to give an account to the judge about why Missy should be able to testify. That was before the agent was killed. I've thought several times about calling her and trying to get her opinion when Missy stopped talking."

"So she didn't stop talking until after the agent was killed? Did she witness it?"

"No, of course not." They'd been huddled in the closet while Penny was trying to call Agent Sinclair for help. It seemed the agent had called for backup too, because the FBI arrived before the assailant found their hiding place. But Missy had been by the door. Had she peeked out and witnessed the murder?

Penny stopped walking as the realization hit her. "She started drawing the man bleeding out on the floor after that. That's also when she stopped speaking." She stared up at Caleb. "No one was murdered during the bank robbery. I tried to keep her from seeing the FBI agent who'd gotten killed but we had no choice but to walk past his body. When Missy started drawing murder scenes, I assumed it was her memory of walking past him—but maybe it's more than that. She must have seen the murder." She bit her lip to keep from crying and Caleb pulled her into his arms. She pressed her face against his chest as tears overwhelmed her. "She saw it, Caleb. She saw a man get murdered." Despite the fact they'd been chased and threatened and nearly killed, she hadn't realized that Missy's main trauma had come when the FBI agent protecting them had been killed in their hotel room. "How could I not have realized it?"

"You and Missy have been through so much. I'm not surprised that it was hard to tell which thing was the last straw that made her shut down and retreat into herself."

She stared up into Caleb's eyes and realized that because of him, that was changing. "She's starting to open up again and that's because of you. She's taken to you. She trusts you, Caleb, and now she trusts Hannah too. She cares about you both."

"That's good because I care for her too." He pushed a hair from her face and his voice lowered. "And for you." His eyes lowered to her lips. He wanted to kiss her and she wanted it too. She leaned in to him instinctively before she caught herself.

She had to keep her head. She couldn't get so swept up in her feelings for this man that she lost sight of what was really important. She pushed away from him before their lips touched. "It is wonderful, Caleb, but it doesn't take away from the trauma she's endured. We need to find a safe place so she can get the emotional help she needs."

He stepped away, his demeanor changing to match her distance.

"I'm sorry, Caleb. I don't want to hurt you."

"No, it's fine."

"Obviously, I am attracted to you and I owe you so much. It's just that I have to think about Missy first. I can't let my emotions color my judgment."

"I understand. Protecting you and Missy is my top priority too. I won't let anything happen to either of you," he told her. "I promise I won't. But...if we can't think about anything else right now when the danger is so high, then it doesn't really leave us with many options, does it? It's not like we can wait until things calm down—because once that happens, you'll be leaving for witness protection. I confess I've been struggling with knowing that once this is all over, you and Missy will be gone and I won't get to see you again. That's going to be harder for me than I'd anticipated."

Tears pressed against her eyelids. He was right. Once this was over and they were safely away in witness protection, she wouldn't see him again. Sadness washed over her at that prospect.

She scrolled through the names on his list again to cover her emotional response. "I'm sorry, Caleb, but there are only a few names that I recognize—and I don't remember anything out of the ordinary about them."

"That's okay. It was a long shot anyway. I was just hoping we could pinpoint how these men are finding you and Missy. I don't understand it. But Luke and Agent Sinclair are still digging into it. They'll figure it out."

She hoped they figured it out soon so she and Missy could enter witness protection. She stole a glance at Caleb and rethought. Maybe not too soon.

"I should get back to the house. I don't begrudge Missy having a good time but I'll feel better being with her."

They turned to walk back but he stopped. "Hey, I have an idea. It's a beautiful day out. Do you think Missy would like to ride the horses?"

Horses! The thought of going horseback riding sent a wave of elation through her. It had been years since she'd been riding. Although it didn't seem like the ideal time, if they were going to be here, taking a ride would be lovely. "I love that idea." Her daughter needed some more lightheartedness in her life. Still, she couldn't help but worry. "But is it safe?"

"It's fine. We'll stay close to the house."

They walked back to the house and entered through the kitchen. It was now empty but the aroma of cookies filled the space. They found Hannah and Missy in the living room where the older woman was reading Missy a book. Penny smiled, loving how normal this scene looked. Hannah could have been any grandmother reading to her granddaughter. She liked the idea that Missy was finally feeling safe again.

"How was your walk?" Hannah asked.

"Wonderful. Caleb is going to take us horseback riding."

"Oh, that sounds like fun." She looked at Missy,

then squeezed her gently. "You're going to have a great time, Missy."

Penny ran to fetch Missy's jacket, then slipped it on while Missy beamed with excitement. She looked like she was ready to speak and Penny waited anxiously, but the words never came. She touched Missy's cheek and blinked back the tears that welled up. She had to be patient.

She took Missy's hand and Caleb held the other as they walked down to the barn. Caleb greeted an older man.

"Hey, Ed." He turned to Penny. "This is Ed. He's been the ranch manager here for as long as I can remember. Ed, this is Penny and her daughter, Missy."

Ed tipped his cowboy hat. "Nice to meet you, ladies."

"We thought we'd take advantage of this beautiful day and go for a ride."

"Sounds good," the older man said.

He went and retrieved two horses and he and Caleb brushed and saddled them up as Missy watched. Her eyes were wide and a light shined in them.

"Do you want to pet him?" Caleb asked, lifting Missy up. He reached out his hand and stroked the horse's nose and encouraged her to do the same.

Penny watched, entranced by the scene before her. If anyone had seen them in this moment, they might have thought they were looking at a father and daughter having a sweet moment. They certainly wouldn't have guessed that Penny and Missy were being hunted down and Caleb was someone they'd only known for a matter of days who was fighting to protect them. It was a simple moment but it meant a lot to Penny to have it. It wasn't often that she'd seen Missy's face show anything but fear and anxiety lately.

"Have you ever ridden?" Caleb asked Penny and she smiled.

"I took riding lessons as a child and owned my own horse until I was fifteen."

"What happened then?"

She shrugged. "I don't know. I reached an age where boys became more important than horses." She felt her face warm at how silly she'd been. "I should have stuck with the horses, I guess, but I would have had to sell her anyway after my mom died."

"I understand. Owning a horse is a big commitment. You probably just outgrew it."

"I never stopped loving her though," she said, stroking the horse's nose.

"This is Snowy. He's real gentle. I'll let you ride him. I'll take Missy with me on Buster Brown." He motioned to the other horse.

She was a little uncertain about letting Missy on a horse without her but if she was trusting Caleb to protect them from the bad guys, she could certainly trust him to keep her safe on a horse. He'd obviously grown up around them and was an experienced rider.

Penny settled into the saddle on Snowy while Caleb climbed onto Buster Brown and Ed lifted Missy up to him. Penny felt a momentary twinge at how adorable they looked. Missy seemed so comfortable with Caleb, a hint of the sweet, affectionate girl she used to be before this nightmare had started.

Caleb started them off down the trail slowly and Penny followed along, getting to know the horse. As they pushed into the open pasture, she had the urge to push the horse into a gallop. She laughed at the freedom she felt being on horseback again. It had been so long and it seemed like her life had only gone downhill since the last time she'd ridden her horse.

Caleb followed behind her, pushing his horse into a gallop, and Penny heard Missy's laughter fill the air. Her heart leapt at the sound. She longed to hear that laughter all the time.

They rode through the pasture and Caleb pointed to something in the distance. "Look over there. Under that row of trees, my cousins and I built a fort when we were kids. We used to go there and hide out from the adults, especially when things got ugly and the adults started arguing."

He rode over to the fort and climbed off the horse, lifting Missy down with him. Penny dismounted and followed them toward the makeshift fort with four walls, a flattop roof and an opening to crawl through. It looked like a chicken coop but without the wire.

He and Missy both got down on their hands and knees to peek inside.

"How long has it been since you've been in there?" Penny asked, wondering what critters might have made it their home since the last time anyone had bothered looking.

He glanced back at her and must have realized her concerns. "A long while." He held out his hand to stop

Missy from darting inside. "Let me make sure it's clear first."

He stuck his head inside, then suddenly started convulsing on the ground. Penny panicked and screamed his name but, before she could do anything else, he stopped and drew his head back out. A grin spread across his face to show them he was only joking. Missy rolled on the ground laughing at his antics and even Penny had to smile.

Yet she couldn't let him off the hook that easily. She nudged his foot. "You scared me."

He laughed, deep and low. "I'm sorry. I was only joking around."

He crawled inside. "It's clear. Come on in."

Missy crawled in and Penny got down on her hands and knees and followed them. It was just a big wooden box, like a treehouse but on the ground. Still, it looked perfect for little kids looking to get away from their troubles. Which made her wonder what kind of troubles little Caleb and his cousins had had growing up on this fancy, opulent ranch.

The space was cramped for two adults however and they were physically closer than she'd expected. She was suddenly very aware of how near Caleb's hand was to hers and how close their faces were to one another.

Her heart began to race at their position but she did her best to shrug it off. Why was she allowing herself to get so rattled by this handsome cowboy? It would be a mistake to let herself lose her heart to him.

Still, as his hand brushed hers, she couldn't ignore the rush of electricity that danced up her arm. She glanced up into his face and felt the tension between them. She could tell that he felt it too. That rush of attraction. She couldn't deny it. He was literally the handsome cowboy who'd swooped to their rescue.

His gaze fell to her lips and she knew he wanted to kiss her. She wanted it too, but it would be a mistake. She was already out on a limb, trusting him as much as she did.

She pulled her hand away and he took the hint and pushed toward the opening. "I suppose we should get back to the house. It'll be time for supper soon enough." Once they were outside the fort and back in the grass, Caleb swooped Missy off her feet. "Are you hungry, little one?"

She nodded as he lifted her up into the saddle. He turned to help Penny up onto the horse and she felt that spark again as he held on to her arm.

"You okay?"

She nodded. "Fine." But she was anything but. Their nice outing had her head spinning with uncertainty. She could lose her life to the bad guys but she could also so easily lose her heart to this kind man.

He climbed back onto Buster Brown and they turned back to the stables.

Once there, Penny unsaddled her horse, then helped brush him down before returning him to his stall. He'd been gentle with her and easy to ride just as Caleb had claimed, and she gave him a good rubdown as thanks.

Caleb did the same with Buster Brown, then walked his horse to the stall.

He handed Missy a carrot. "Want to feed Buster Brown a treat?"

She nodded and he held her up. She fed the horse, then rubbed his nose and kissed it. "Good night, Buster Brown."

Penny's heart leapt at her simple statement and Caleb looked at her, surprised. Tears filled Penny's eyes. It was the first words she'd heard her daughter speak in months. She pressed a hand to her mouth to hold back a squeal of joy but she wanted to shout to the sky.

Caleb bounced her happily, then put his arm around Penny's shoulder and pulled her close as they walked back to the house.

She leaned into him, enjoying the feeling of happiness that spread through her.

Her daughter was talking again and it was because of this man.

The sound of Missy speaking was music to Caleb's ears. He tried not to make a big deal out of it to not embarrass her, yet he saw tears form in Penny's eyes.

He kept his arm around Penny as they walked back to the house. He carried Missy but she soon squirmed away and ran ahead of them. As they reached the back door and Missy darted inside, Penny pulled on his arm to stop him. He turned to see why and lovely, soft lips met his.

He wrapped his arms around her and kissed her back.

It ended way too soon for his liking but this time, unlike their previous almost-kisses, her eyes weren't clouded with regret. She wasn't sorry and neither was he. Not for one moment.

"Thank you, Caleb," she whispered, her fingers still clinging to his arms. "Thank you."

His mind was spinning so he wasn't exactly sure what she was thanking him for at that moment. "I didn't do anything."

"Yes, you did. You've done so much more than keep Missy and me safe. You've made us *feel* safe. You've brought us back to life."

It was nothing compared to what they'd done for him. Somehow, Penny had managed to open up his heart to love. That was something he'd never believed possible. He stroked her hair, then gently placed a kiss on her forehead as he drew her to him. It was no use fighting it any longer. His feelings for this woman had grown into something he could no longer deny. He loved her.

"I don't know how this is all going to end, Penny. All I know is that I don't want to lose you. I want you to stay. I want to be with you. I want to build a family with you and Missy. I don't really know how it happened, but I'm crazy about you and I don't want to let either one of you go."

She smiled up at him but her expression quickly turned wistful. "I wish things were different. I love this place and I wish Missy and I could stay here, but I don't know how that would even be possible."

He shook his head. "Neither do I, until we figure out who is leaking your location."

"Once you do, Missy and I will go into witness protection."

It was the best thing for them in order to keep them safe long-term, but it meant he would never see them again. Even knowing that was coming was a twist to his heart. "I wish things were different. I want things to be different." It wasn't fair that he'd finally found a woman he could love and she was destined to be taken from him.

"Me too, but they aren't." She kissed him one more time before pulling away from him. "I've come to care a lot about you, Caleb, but our lives are moving in two complete opposite directions. We can never have a future together."

The truth in her words gutted him. He'd never opened his heart to anyone before and now doing so was backfiring on him. His only choice to truly keep her safe once this immediate threat was over was to let her go. He pressed his forehead against hers. "It's not fair," he told her.

"It's not," she agreed. "But it's what we have to do." She reached up and stroked his cheek. "You will always be the man who rescued us in every way you could."

He opened the back door and stood back while she stepped inside, wiping tears from her cheeks. It was heartbreaking to know they could never be together but, for now, they needed to focus on the good things, like Missy being vocal again.

Missy ran to Penny as they walked through the kitchen. "Look, Mama, cookies!" She held up a plate of the cookies she and Hannah had put in the oven before their outing. "That's wonderful, baby," Penny said, pulling her into a hug again.

The little girl pulled away from her, grabbed a cookie, then ran into the living room.

Penny reached out to touch Hannah's arm. "Thank you," she whispered before following her daughter out of the room.

Hannah waited until they were out of earshot before she turned to Caleb. "She's talking! When did that happen?"

"Just a few minutes ago when we returned from riding the horses. It's incredible."

"What a blessing," Hannah agreed. "I'm so happy to see that little girl beginning to heal from all she's been through."

He sighed and leaned across the island. "It is wonderful, but she might revert again if Luke and I can't figure out how to keep her safe."

Hannah gave him a reassuring pat on the arm. "You will. You're a good cop, Caleb—and you've always come through for the people who matter to you. I can tell how much you care for them."

"I do care for them. More than I should."

"Caring is never wrong, Caleb."

"It is when you know there's no future for you."

Hannah reached for his hands. "None?"

"Their best chance at remaining safe is witness protection. I'll never see them again."

She sighed and frowned at him. "I'm so sorry, honey. I know this must be so difficult for you. It's the first time you've put your heart out there."

"Unfortunately, what's best for me and what's best for them are two different things. When the time comes, I'm going to have to let them go. But how do I do that when all I want is for them to stay?"

She gave him a motherly hug and he wrapped his arms around her. "I guess all you can do is enjoy the time you can spend with them until they enter the program. Why don't you go hang out with them? I'll be fixing supper soon. We can all eat together."

"What would I do without you, Hannah?"

A smile spread across her face. "I don't know. Thankfully, you'll never have to find out."

He wandered into the living room where he found Penny curled up on the couch and Missy coloring on the coffee table. He took the seat beside her. "How is she?" he asked in a low voice so Missy wouldn't overhear.

"She's good. Thanks to you."

And thanks to her and Missy, this house that he'd lived in for most of his life was finally starting to feel like home. He didn't want to see them leave either but he wanted nothing more than to end the threat against them.

He walked over and sat beside Missy on the floor. She was drawing horses now—a white horse and a brown one. "That's Buster Brown," she proudly told him.

"That looks just like him." It was good to see her drawing happy images for once.

However, the pages on the floor included one with the same old drawing—a uniformed man with a gun standing over a dead person, blood spread out around him.

He'd hoped they would have gotten past this by now. He rubbed his chin as he picked up the image and looked at it. Missy got up and slipped into his lap, putting her arms around his neck. He looked at her and as she smiled at him, a swell of emotion caught in his throat.

It wasn't just the beautiful mother sitting a few inches away that he'd fallen for. This little girl with her pigtails and toothy smile had also stolen his heart. He wanted more days like today for her. More smiles. More laughter. More drawing of horses and clouds instead of doom and gloom.

She wouldn't have that until these threats against her were neutralized.

He stared at the drawing. The fact that she felt compelled to draw it over and over had him more and more convinced that she must have witnessed the agent's murder that night in the hotel. But then why was the killer wearing a uniform? And why had she only started drawing the uniform and badge on the killer since she'd met him?

Now that she was speaking again, he could finally ask her. He picked up the drawing. "Missy, can I ask why you keep drawing me in these pictures? I wasn't there, you know."

She looked at him, then at the drawing, and pointed to the man in the uniform. The man with the gun. "He's a bad man."

He pointed to the man in the uniform. "Who is this? Is this me?"

She shook her head and pointed to him again. "He's the bad man."

She crawled from his lap and returned to her spot on the floor to keep drawing clouds over the horses.

All this time, he'd thought Missy was drawing him,

pulling him and his uniform into her drawings as a way to cope. But if this man—this killer—wasn't him, then who was he? Was this an image from the crime scene at the bank robbery? But no, no one had been shot during that robbery. Was it possible she'd seen a policeman standing over the body of the FBI agent after he was killed? No, because Penny had loaded her up and left the scene once the police and FBI agents arrived.

Had the killer then been a police officer? Law enforcement had its share of bad people just like any profession, but he found it hard to believe that a patrol officer from Kentucky would murder an FBI agent. Or that he'd wear his uniform while doing so.

But who else would she have seen in uniform that she would believe was a bad man?

Suddenly, it hit him. They were looking for someone who hadn't been on their radar.

"I have to go," he told Penny. "I'll be at the police station if you need me."

"What is it?"

"I might have figured out something really important." He kissed her, lingering on her lips for a second longer than he knew he should. "Keep inside with Hannah. I'll call you if my hunch pans out."

He hurried out the door, hollering at Hannah that he was leaving. He also set the security alarm, then called Ed to let him know to keep the gates secure. He still had the ranch hands on alert and Caleb would have an officer sent out to keep watch. He wasn't taking any chances with Penny and Missy's safety but he couldn't ignore

# ELEVEN

Caleb hurried into the police station and toward the conference room.

Luke was waiting for him when he arrived. "What's going on? What did you find?"

He held out the drawing Missy had made. "See this man?" He pointed to the guy in uniform standing over the dead body with a gun. "Penny said she didn't start drawing the uniform until they met me, so I thought Missy was drawing me, pulling me into her trauma to try to deal with it."

"You killing the bad guy?"

"Right. Only that's not me. She told me so tonight. She said this man in uniform was a bad man."

"Wait." Luke frowned and held up his hand. "She's talking?"

"Yes, she's started speaking again today. I took her down to the stables and we rode the horses and scoped out the old fort."

"That thing is still standing?"

"Barely," Caleb told him. "Honestly, we had a great afternoon and we went back to the stables and she spoke to the horse. Then in the kitchen with Hannah, she did it again."

"That's incredible."

"I know. It's amazing and Penny and I were both in awe. She says it's because Missy feels safe at the ranch that she's finally starting to open up again."

"You don't want them to leave, do you?"

He took a deep breath to settle the emotion that caught in his throat. He shook his head. "No, I don't. I don't want to give them up. I will though, if that will keep them safe." But, if they could identify this man Missy was drawing, they might be able to bring down the entire operation and keep Penny and Missy safe once for all.

"Anyways, like I was telling you—I asked her about the drawing, and she said it wasn't me. She said it was a bad man."

He stared at the drawing and Caleb could see his cousin trying to piece things together. "I don't remember the report about the bank robbery mentioning that any of the bank robbers were in a uniform. Plus no one was killed at the bank."

"Right, but if she saw him at the bank in his uniform, then saw him again when he was murdering the FBI agent a few days later, then maybe this is her way of telling us who it was. She's trying to say the man who killed the agent was at the bank in his uniform."

"So who is it?"

"The only one at the bank who was wearing a police-like uniform. The bank's security guard."

Luke dug through a stack of files until he pulled out the list of victims at the bank that day. "According to the officer who took his statement after the robbery, he was pretty shaken up by the whole thing. You think he could be involved in the robbery and the murder?"

"That's what I'm thinking. He could have faked his reaction after the robbery. Everyone would be looking for the robbers, not one of the victims who worked there. Did the FBI perform a background check on him?"

"Of course. They did checks on all the people inside the bank. That's standard operating procedure. It's not unheard of for criminals to have someone on the inside scoping out the place before the actual crime. The Bureau background checks everyone." Luke grabbed his laptop and dug through the files. "Here it is. The security guard's name was Stu Stafford. He had a clean background. No criminal record. Employee records show he started working at the bank a few weeks before it was robbed."

"So maybe he was scoping it out for the others. Where did he work previously?"

Luke shook his head. "He's had multiple dead-end jobs but I don't see anything that points to him being involved. Do you recognize him as the man who attacked you at the fishing cabin?"

He stared at the image. "Well, he's the right build and height, but I can't say for certain. That guy was wearing a mask over his face. None of us got a good look at him."

"No, but we have his blood," Luke reminded him. "The crime scene crew went there and processed the scene after the attack, remember? By the way, Jefferson and some of the others want to know if you'd be willing to rent the place out on weekends for fishing trips."

He'd forgotten they'd sent the crime scene crew. "They were able to collect the attacker's blood?"

Luke nodded. "They spotted a trail of it. It's not much, but we're sending it off for DNA testing."

"That's still going to take a while to get back and that's assuming our killer's DNA is in the system. According to the FBI's background check, Stu doesn't have a criminal record." Caleb sighed and ran a hand through his hair. "I suppose the best way to figure out if my hunch is right is to see if Missy can identify Stafford." But, if he was right, would seeing the face of the killer cause her to revert back to being nonverbal? She was going to have to identify him and the other robbers eventually in court, but what he wouldn't give for a child psychologist on speed dial right about now.

He thought about Dr. Williams, the child psychologist that the FBI had hired to evaluate Missy's readiness to testify. "I wonder if Dr. Williams could give us some suggestions for making sure I don't hurt Missy's progress."

"You're assuming she'll be traumatized if she sees him again because you're assuming this is the guy she saw kill that federal agent at their hotel."

"Will she be traumatized? It seems pretty likely. Is this the same guy? I don't know—but it sounds right to me. Call it a gut feeling, but who else has she seen in uniform that she would call a bad man?" He pulled out his cell phone. "Maybe I can look up the doctor's number."

"No need," Luke stated. "I'm sure her information is listed in the file." He dug through it and found the information he needed. "I'll e-mail her and see if she can do a video chat with us to answer your questions."

Caleb hurried to his office and grabbed his laptop to perform a deep dive on Stu Stafford while they waited to hear back from the doctor. Instinct was telling him this was the man who was the real threat to Missy and Penny. Now, he just had to prove it. And, once he figured that out, they could uncover who in the FBI or the Marshals' office was funneling him information about Penny and Missy.

Unfortunately, he got nowhere on his investigation into Stafford. The man had led an uneventful life, jumping from job to job with no stable home address or phone number. His online history was skimpy. He seemed to prefer to stay under the radar. As Luke had stated, he had no criminal background. He didn't even have much of a credit history.

He closed his laptop, frustrated by his efforts. He was no closer to proving Stu Stafford was the killer than he had been earlier. Everything was riding on Missy being able to identify him.

He pulled out his cell phone and called Penny, finding himself smiling at the sound of her voice when she answered.

"Did your hunch pan out?" she asked him.

"I'm not sure yet. I think the man in the picture that Missy has been drawing is the bank's security guard—a man named Stu Stafford. I think he was involved in the robbery and then killed the agent protecting you both.

He might also be the man who attacked us at the cabin. The forensics team found blood from where I shot him but it will be weeks before that's back, and unless he's in the system—which it doesn't seem like he is—we won't be able to match it anyway."

"So what are you going to do?"

"I want to see if Missy can identify him. But she's made so much progress, I don't want to frighten her and make her regress again."

"I don't want that either. I barely even remember the security guard at the bank. I know he spoke to Missy when we walked in. Back then, she would talk to anyone."

"If he is part of the bank robbery ring, he could be the one hiring the men who initially attacked you— with him coming to town himself later to get the job done. Only, I don't have any other way to prove it's him though. I've requested a call with Dr. Williams, the child psychologist you saw after the robbery. I'm hoping she can give me some help in getting the identification from Missy without frightening her."

"So you really need her to identify him?" He heard the hesitation in her voice and hated that he was putting them through this, but there were no other choices he could come up with.

"Yes. Are you okay with that?"

"Well, I don't like it. Like you, I'm worried about it being triggering for Missy, but if we can put this man away it means she'll be safe. It's a risk we have to take."

They'd already taken so many risks already and he hated to add another one to their plate, but he didn't know what else to do. If Stafford was involved with the ring and was the one behind the attacks against Penny and Missy, he needed to be stopped.

Only, Caleb had also found no indication that Stafford had any connections with the FBI or Marshals' office. There was no evidence that anyone in either agency was feeding him information about their whereabouts. So then how had he found them when he shouldn't have been able to? How had he found Penny and Missy in Texas in the first place?

That still gnawed at him.

He spotted his deputy chief hovering outside his door and wrapped up his call with Penny. "I'm still waiting to hear from Dr. Williams. I'll call you once I do and let you know what she says."

He ended the call, then waved Morrison into his office.

"I don't mean to interrupt, Chief."

"It's no problem. I'm in limbo, waiting for someone to call us back. What's up?"

"There's something I think you need to see."

He took the sheet of paper from Morrison and looked at it. "It's a lab report." He noticed the name—Chet Harmon. "It's a lab report about my grandfather. Where did you get this?"

"Someone from the medical examiner's office e-mailed it to me. Apparently, it got lost in their files and was never sent over."

He noticed the date. It was after his grandfather's death, which meant it must have been a lab performed during his autopsy. "Okay, so it needs to be added to his case file." It seemed there was a clerical error that had now been rectified. He didn't understand what the big deal was.

"This report shows your grandfather's blood levels were abnormal. Basically, it proves that your grandfather didn't die from a heart attack. He was murdered."

His words stopped Caleb cold. His grandpa Chet had died almost a year ago. They'd already had the funeral and begun divvying up the estate. How could it be that no one had realized this sooner? "The medical examiner at the time determined he died from natural causes. I have a copy of the death certificate."

"She never saw this. Like I said, this report fell through the cracks. They had some upheaval at the office and they now have a new medical examiner. She's changing the official cause of death from natural causes to homicide. They sent it back to our office to investigate."

Luke poked his head into Caleb's office. "Dr. Williams can video call with us in twenty minutes."

He acknowledged Luke's comment, then turned back to Morrison. "There wasn't much of an investigation done when my grandfather died because we all presumed it was natural causes. He was an old man after all. But pull whatever files you can find and leave them on my desk. I'll look it over when I can." His grandfather wasn't going anywhere and he was still trying to wrap his head around the idea of him being killed anyway. He had to keep his focus on Penny and Missy for now. He would deal with this unexpected homicide investigation once this was over and they were safe.

He hurried into the conference room. He must have looked grim because Luke shot him a look. "Are you okay?"

He didn't have the time to explain this new hiccup to his cousin. "It has nothing to do with this case. I'll catch you up later."

Luke didn't press him and it was a good thing because the psychologist called in just then.

Caleb pressed the answer key on the computer and a professional-looking woman popped up on the screen. "Dr. Williams, I'm Chief Caleb Harmon of the Jessup Police Department in Jessup, Texas. This is my cousin, retired FBI agent Luke Harmon. Thank you for agreeing to speak with us."

After the greetings, she got right to business. "You said in your e-mail that this was in reference to Missy Jackson? She's the child that was the prime witness in the bank robbery case here in Kentucky, correct?"

"That's right. I don't know if you are aware, but the FBI agent who was protecting her and her mother was murdered. Missy witnessed it. It caused her to shut down. She stopped speaking for a time."

Surprise filled the woman's face and she started nervously toying with the charm around her neck and clearing her throat. "I wasn't aware of that. That must have occurred after I had my consultation with her. All I knew about was the bank robbery and I was prepared to tell the judge that she was competent to testify, despite her age. I'd wondered why the hearing kept getting pushed back."

"Missy and her mother became targets after the bank

robbery. That was when they were put under protective custody—and when the agent guarding them was killed. After the agent was killed, Penny took her daughter and ran. She ended up here in Texas with us but she's still got people coming after her, trying to stop Missy from testifying."

"I see. And how is Missy dealing with all of this?"

"Well, after she witnessed the murder, she stopped speaking and started drawing terrible images. But lately, she's doing better. She's started speaking again. The problem is that I have an idea about who might be behind these attacks. I want to ask her to identify him but I'm worried seeing him again might cause her to regress. I was hoping you could give me some guidance."

"You know who was behind everything?"

"I have a hunch. I need her to confirm it."

She continued to fiddle with her necklace, a clear indication that she was agitated. "Who do you believe it is?"

Luke shot him an odd look. Dr. Williams was acting more nervous than was called for. "Is something wrong, Dr. Williams?"

She shook her head. "No, no. I'm just curious about the investigation."

Luke grabbed another laptop and started typing furiously. Caleb could tell he was on to something but he motioned for Caleb to keep going with Dr. Williams.

He pulled out the last drawing Missy had done and showed it to her. She gasped at the sight, which surprised him. It seemed like a very unprofessional response. This drawing couldn't have been the most disturbing thing she'd seen in her practice, especially if she frequently worked with children who had witnessed crimes to assess their capability to testify.

She grimaced. "Missy drew that?"

"Yes. According to her mother, she's been drawing things like this since the agent was killed. Recently, she started drawing the killer in uniform. At first, I thought she was drawing me, but she told me this was the bad man. The only uniformed man she would have encountered during the bank robbery was the security guard. I'm thinking that perhaps she saw my uniform and remembered he was wearing one at the bank and added it to her drawings."

Luke turned the other laptop around and Caleb saw the screen was showing a social media site belonging to the doctor. At first, he was confused about what his cousin was showing him until Luke pointed to the name at the top.

Anna Stafford Williams.

Stafford? As in Stu Stafford?

That revelation shook Caleb. He turned back to Dr. Williams. "The man I believe murdered a federal agent and sent Missy and Penny running for their lives is named Stu Stafford."

He saw her grimace at the name and knew they'd hit on something.

"Have you heard of him?"

He could see she was visibly shaken now. "I'm sorry but I can't help you." She started to disconnect, but Caleb stopped her.

"Dr. Williams, if you end this call now, I'll simply

contact Agent Sinclair of the FBI. She'll be at your office in a matter of minutes. Trust me—you won't be able to avoid answering her questions. Now, how do you know Stu Stafford?"

She bit her lip, then gave up the charade. "He's my half brother and he's a menace. When he discovered I was consulting with the FBI on this case, he threatened my family."

"What did he want from you?"

He wished they were in the same room so he could press her as she hesitated to admit what she'd done. Stafford had clearly demanded and gotten her assistance in some way.

"What did he want from you, Dr. Williams?"

"He wanted me to tell the judge that Missy didn't have the maturity to testify."

"But that didn't happen."

"No, the Attorney General refused to accept my determination. They wanted me to change my recommendation. When I refused, they decided to consult with someone else. When Stu learned I wasn't going to be able to help him and his associates with the judge, he had me do one more thing for him. I didn't want to do it but he threatened my kids." Her tone raised, indicating she was working hard to justify herself and her actions.

It couldn't be good.

"What did he want you to do?"

"He wanted me to go see Missy and to give her something. It was a toy. A stuffed monkey to be exact."

His gut clenched. Missy was attached to that toy—he'd seen as much himself. "Why would he give her that?"

"He said the FBI was hiding the little girl. The monkey had a tracker inside it. I had no idea that he was going to kill anyone. I didn't even know he had until you just told me so. I promise you—I didn't know. I was only trying to protect my family."

Caleb bit back a bitter response. "What did you think he was going to do once he found her?"

She sighed. "Honestly, I tried not to think about it."

So that explained how they'd been found even at the remote cabin. The bad guys had been tracking them all this time. He doubted the tracker had a long range since it had taken days for the bad guys to find them at the cabin…unless they'd been specifically waiting for Stafford to arrive in town to handle it himself.

He glanced at Luke whose face was grim as he picked up the phone. "I'm calling Agent Sinclair right now," he told Dr. Williams. "And you'll tell her just what you told us."

Caleb ended the call, angry that this woman had compromised the safety and security of a little girl, especially since it was her job to help kids.

A few minutes later, Luke turned back to Caleb. "Agent Sinclair is on her way to Dr. Williams's office. She'll take her in for questioning and then they'll track down Stafford. I guess you don't need Missy to identify him now that Dr. Williams can provide testimony against him for murder and witness tampering."

But Caleb was focused on something else Dr. Williams had said. "He placed a tracker inside Missy's toy."

Luke nodded at that. "That was a risk. What if, when she ran, she didn't take it with her?"

"But she did. He's been tracking them all this time. That's how he's been finding her and sending people after them."

And Caleb had left them alone at the ranch.

The idea that this maniac knew where they were was disturbing.

He took a breath, remembering that she wasn't alone. Hannah was with them, as were Ed and the ranch hands. But Stafford had murdered an FBI agent and a US Marshal. He was extremely dangerous and working hard to tie up loose ends.

He dialed the cell phone he'd given Penny.

No answer.

Hannah had promised to remain with them, but she always turned off her cell phone when she was at the ranch and used the landline. So he called the house phone, but no one answered there either.

That didn't bode well.

He called Officer Dale Mason next. He'd tasked Mason with standing guard at the front entrance of the ranch.

He answered but didn't provide much information. "I haven't seen or heard anything out of the ordinary," Mason told him when Caleb mentioned his concerns.

But something still wasn't sitting right with Caleb. "I'm on my way there now." He pushed to his feet and spoke to Luke. "No one's answering the phone at the ranch. I've got to get back to them."

If Stafford knew where they were all this time, then that meant he was just waiting for an opportunity to get to them.

\* \* \*

Penny couldn't remember the last time she was so content. Sure, the danger was still out there, but they'd spent the afternoon baking cookies for Hannah's church bake sale and Missy had been smiling and laughing all afternoon. It was the best day they'd had in a long time. Although they'd only been here a short while, Harmon Ranch was beginning to feel like home. She didn't allow herself a second to think about having to leave it. She was enjoying the moment too much.

Hannah popped a second tray of cookies into the oven, then helped Missy wash her hands before ushering her back into the living room to watch a movie. Penny was so thankful for Hannah, who'd stepped up to protect Missy both physically and emotionally. "This batch will be ready before you know it and then we'll decorate them," she told Missy, who smiled and whooped with joy.

Penny watched her hop around the living room and switch on the television. It was a far cry from the silent, solemn little girl who'd been drawing pictures of murder scenes.

"She's a sweet child," Hannah said, touching Penny's shoulder. "You're doing a good job with her."

"Thank you." Tears welled up in her eyes. She needed to hear the reassurance that she wasn't permanently messing up Missy's life. She was doing the best she could by her daughter in uncertain times.

Hannah microwaved a bowl of popcorn and together they all sat and started the movie as the aroma of cookies baking in the oven spilled into the living room.

"I appreciate how you've accepted us into the house," she told Hannah, keeping her voice low so as not to disturb Missy who was enthralled by the movie. "I hope we're not putting anyone out by being here."

"Of course not. This is Caleb's home. He's welcome to have whomever he likes to stay. There's certainly plenty of room." She looked at Penny and gave her a knowing smile. "Besides, I'm glad to see him finally opening up to someone."

"What do you mean?"

Her eyes widened and, for a moment, she grew flustered, as if she had spoken out of turn. "Never mind. It's nothing."

"No, please tell me. I… I'd like to know more about him. I appreciate everything Caleb has done for us. I don't know what would have happened to us if he hadn't intervened."

"Caleb has a heart for helping others. He always has. I'm glad to see he's broadening his reach. Although, I've never seen him get this involved in helping someone. You two must be very special."

Penny felt her face warm. "We're not special."

"Well, there must be something about you. I can see you're pretty but a pretty face has never been everything to Caleb. He's always been so guarded."

That grabbed her attention. "Guarded? What do you mean?"

"Oh, ignore me. I'm just a silly old woman. I've known Caleb since he was a little boy. I've watched his ups and downs. I've seen him get his heart broken and I've watched him wall up his heart so he wouldn't get hurt again."

So that explained why he looked so sad sometimes and why he seemed to be trying to keep his distance from her even as he insisted he wanted to help them. "What do you mean? When did he get his heart broken?"

"Oh, early on. He lost his father. Then his mother abandoned him here. I'm afraid it wasn't an easy life for him. I did my best to help him, to be a mother to him, but he was so hurt by his real mom. After that, he never could truly open his heart to someone else."

"His mother abandoned him?"

"She did. Showed up one day, dropped him off and just never came back. He cried himself to sleep every night for months. Poor little guy was only twelve years old and had just lost his father. She couldn't handle being a single parent so her choice was to leave him here. Maybe she thought she would come back for him one day, but she never did."

"Did he ever see her again?"

"She called on birthdays and holidays for a while and would drop in, but eventually she just stopped. I don't even remember the last time Caleb saw her. I know he hasn't spoken to her in years. I don't think he's trusted any woman since then. I know he loves me, but even with me he doesn't really trust."

That explained his insistence that Penny was special and that not every mother would do whatever it took to protect their child. She looked at her daughter and shuddered. Even in the worst of times, she couldn't imagine leaving her. "That's terrible. I can't imagine abandoning my child. I'm in this mess because I refuse to give up on my daughter."

She smiled. "I like that. That's probably why Caleb likes you too."

She felt her face warm at that sentiment and thought about that kiss she'd shared with him. "I really can't think about relationships right now. That's the last thing on my mind."

"Sometimes romance finds you when you least expect it."

She wasn't sure she had the best track record with romance, given her terrible marriage. Frankly, she wasn't sure she was the best judge of character. Caleb seemed wonderful, but how well did she really know him? Maybe she'd be better off letting their relationship come to its natural end rather than taking the risk of trying for something more. She couldn't really afford to take any more big chances at the moment. Not when her main focus was on getting to a safe place, getting their lives back on track and finding help for Missy's trauma.

"Well, you're welcome here. I'm glad to see Caleb making a change."

"We won't be staying long," Penny insisted. "He's trying to get us into witness protection, then we'll be gone."

Hannah's face twisted. "Then he'll be alone again. I know I'm not his mother but I've practically raised that boy since the day his mother dropped him off here. I want to see good things for him, but he's so resistant to letting anyone in." She shook her head with a sigh, then said, "Guess I'd better go and check that batch of cookies."

Missy saw her stand and started to follow her into the kitchen, but the older woman stopped her. "They'll still have to cool. I'll let you know when they're ready for you to decorate them."

Missy went back to watching the screen. Penny thought about the things Hannah had just told her. They made a lot of sense and explained some things about Caleb and his determination to help them. Did he see in her everything his own mother rejected? Somehow, it made him more endearing to her. Her heart broke at the idea that sometime soon she would have to say goodbye to her handsome cowboy protector. The more she got to know him, the more she wished for a different outcome for them.

Hannah hummed as she headed for the kitchen but her humming suddenly became a cry that ended abruptly. Penny pushed to her feet as a thump sounded from the kitchen. It sounded like someone falling.

She headed toward the kitchen but stopped, her heart racing when she spotted Hannah's feet sticking out from the kitchen doorway. She was on the ground. Had she passed out or had a medical emergency? Penny started to run to her but the sight of a figure standing over Hannah had her backtracking.

The man glanced up at her, then smirked and turned to face her. She hadn't remembered him before, but she recognized him now as the security guard at the bank from the day of the robbery.

Stu Stafford. The man Missy had seen murder a federal agent.

Now, he was here to kill her.

Penny turned and ran, screaming at her daughter. "Run, baby. They found us. Run."

Missy's eyes grew wide with fear but she jumped to her feet without hesitation and darted to the front door. Stafford shoved Penny aside, pulled out a gun and fired.

Penny screamed, fear boiling over into rage at this man shooting at her child. She jumped on him, trying to grab his arm to stop him. He fired off two more shots, but it was too late. Missy was already out the door.

He pushed Penny, trying to get her off him, but she wasn't going to let him go after Missy. Not without a fight. Unfortunately, he wasn't giving up without a fight either. He wasn't much bigger than Penny but he was strong. She held on to his arm but couldn't contain him. He shoved and the gun went off.

Pain ripped through her side as she stumbled backward and fell onto the couch. She gripped her side and groaned in pain.

"Now, stay down," Stafford warned her.

He ran to the door to go after Missy. There was nothing Penny could do to stop him. She could only hope that she had fought long enough for Missy to run to safety.

It seemed her wish was answered, as her assailant turned back and stood over her, then pulled her to him and pressed a gun to her head. The pain in her side was momentarily lessened by the fear of dying on his whim. "Call her back."

Her fear subsided. He needed her to find Missy, but nothing he could do to her would make her help him. She locked eyes with him and jutted out her chin. "No, I won't do it."

He stared her down, then pressed his hand against her wound. Pain took her breath away. "I said call her back. Tell her everything is fine. Make her believe it."

Through the window, she saw Missy disappear behind the barn. Relief flooded her. Relief that her daughter had gotten away. She could hide until help arrived, until Caleb returned and found her. Penny would probably be dead by that time, but the thought didn't scare her—not if Missy would be safe. And as long as she was alive, she wasn't going to help this man abduct and murder her child.

"I would rather die than let you get your hands on my daughter."

He grabbed her chin and turned her face to him, his expression snarled with rage. "That can be arranged," he assured her, pure evil dripping from his every word.

He shoved her back onto the couch but she fell and hit her chin on the coffee table. She tasted blood, but it was nothing compared to what he would probably do to her in order to make her comply. Yet it didn't matter what he did. She wouldn't help him find Missy.

She stole a glance into the kitchen doorway. Hannah's legs were still protruding. Still unmoving. Penny didn't know if she was dead or simply unconscious, but she knew they were both in a very perilous situation.

And, if this man found Missy, her daughter would be killed.

Stafford grabbed her arm and pulled her back to her feet, then toward the door. The pain from her side nearly made her double over but he forced her to keep moving, dragging her outside.

"I'm ready to end this. Let's go find your daughter."

# TWELVE

Caleb flew home, breaking the speed limit as he swerved through the streets toward the ranch. He had tried calling the phones again and again but no one answered. Luke sat beside him, trying all the numbers again. No one was answering and that made him panic.

Caleb turned the truck and pulled in beneath the overhanging sign that announced they were entering Harmon Ranch and Mason followed them in. Everything looked the same. The horses were grazing in the corral as they passed by but he didn't see anyone working in the barn or stables, which struck him as odd.

He parked nearly at the front door, then hopped from the pickup and ran inside. The front door was standing open.

"Penny! Penny, where are you?" He glanced into the living room and spotted blood on the couch. His gut clenched. Something terrible had happened here.

Luke and Mason followed behind him and were stopped by the blood as well. "We'll find her," Luke told Caleb. "No body means she's still alive." He swatted his hands in the air. "What's that smell?"

Only then did Caleb notice the smoke stinging his eyes and the way the smoke alarm was squealing. Something was burning.

They ran into the kitchen. Smoke was billowing out of the oven. He hurried over, opened it, grabbed a pair of oven mitts, then pulled out a tray of little hunks of what he was certain was supposed to be cookies Hannah had been baking for her church. He tossed them into the sink, shut off the oven and waved away smoke that had filled the room as Luke pulled down the smoke alarm to stop it from beeping.

Where were Penny and Missy and Hannah, and what could have happened to make them abandon their baking? Dread filled him.

Suddenly, through the smoke, Caleb spotted a figure on the floor. His heart leapt into his throat as he rushed over and knelt beside her. "Hannah! It's Hannah!"

Luke hurried over too. The housekeeper had a gash on the back of her head and blood was oozing from it. Luke checked for a pulse. "She's unconscious but she's alive."

"But where is everyone else?"

"I'll check the rest of the house," Mason said, then ran from the room.

Dread filled Caleb's gut. Penny wouldn't have left Hannah if she'd had a choice. Someone had broken in and done this. But had they gotten Penny and Missy too or were the mother and daughter hiding? If they were still alive, where were they?

Luke's calmer head prevailed. "Why don't you check

the security feeds? I'll call for backup and an ambulance for Hannah."

That was a good idea. Caleb raced to the security room. His grandfather had been security conscious, which was one reason Caleb had felt safe bringing Penny and Missy here. He had cameras in place to cover most of the outside areas surrounding the house and barns.

Caleb pulled up the video feeds and replayed them until he spotted the front door swinging open and Missy running out. She darted down the driveway and around the barn. Even though he couldn't see her face, the way she moved told him everything he needed to know.

She had been running for her life.

He gritted his teeth at his worst fears coming to life. Stafford had found them again.

He fast-forwarded until he spotted movement in the doorway once again. A man had Penny by the arm, a gun to her side, and was shoving her out the door. Even on the monitor, he could see she was pale and struggled to walk. Caleb switched to the barn feeds and watched them follow the same route Missy had gone, then disappear behind the barn, Stafford pulling her along with him.

He clenched his fists at seeing that and knowing he hadn't been there to stop it. They should have been safe here at the ranch.

Why hadn't they been? Hannah had obviously been attacked before she could grab for a weapon. He must have surprised them. But where were Ed and the ranch hands? They were supposed to have been watching the gates for intruders.

He switched feeds again and got his answer. Ed was tied up inside his office in the barn. The assailant must have surprised him.

So much for them being safe at the ranch.

Caleb hurried back into the kitchen. Hannah was moaning and his heart jumped with relief. "How is she?" he asked Luke.

"She's just waking up. I called for an ambulance. Did you see anything on the video?"

"He dragged Penny out past the barn at gunpoint. I think they might be looking for Missy. She ran from the house a few minutes before them. Also, Ed is tied up in the shed. I have no idea where everyone else is."

Mason came barreling down the stairs. "The rest of the house is clear."

The sound of a vehicle pulling up grabbed their attention. Caleb reached for his gun and Luke followed suit as they headed for the window. Luke stopped him before they reached the front door, motioning to the window that showed Luke's wife getting out of the car.

Caleb hadn't even thought about her showing up. He felt his stomach twist at the thought of the danger she was in. He put away his gun as she entered through the side door.

Abby walked inside and coughed at the lingering smoke, then spotted Hannah on the floor. "What happened?"

"Someone broke into the house. He took Penny and went searching for Missy in the pasture," Luke explained. "Hannah was attacked."

"I have to go after them," Caleb said and Luke nodded, then turned to Abby.

"I've already called for an ambulance and backup. When they arrive, send them out there."

She nodded and waved them away. "Go. I'll lock the door behind you. We'll be fine. Go help them."

"I'll stay with them until the ambulance and backup arrives," Mason stated.

Caleb was relieved to have Luke by his side. He would have gone alone, but he was glad for the backup in facing this man who was threatening to take those he loved most away from him.

Yes, he loved her. He could finally admit that now—when it might be too late.

They hurried down the path that led to the barn and cleared the area before finding and untying Ed. The man was madder than all get-out at being surprised and overtaken, but he was mostly worried about Penny and Missy.

"How did he get the best of you?" Caleb asked Ed.

"One of the ranch hands saw a brush fire out by the west fence. The others had to go help put it out. After they left, the man showed up. He had Penny at gunpoint," Ed told them. "I had no choice but to do what he said. He locked me in my office. Said he was going to shut up the girl once and for all. I knew then that the fire must have been a trap to sneak onto the ranch and lure the others away but I couldn't do anything about it. I'm sorry, Caleb. I let you down."

"It's okay," Luke assured him. "We'll find them."

They headed behind the barn, guns raised, until

Caleb spotted Penny on the other side of the fence in the open field. In the distance, smoke churned up against the blue sky. The fire Stafford had started. But Caleb couldn't focus on that at the moment. A man he recognized as Stu Stafford, the security guard from the bank robbery, was holding a gun on Penny.

He glanced at Luke who nodded at him, indicating he'd seen them. Caleb moved left while Luke moved right, circling around them as they moved closer. Caleb took cover behind an old tractor that had long since broken down. Penny and Stafford were standing in an open field so he and Luke couldn't sneak up on him. This was going to come down to a confrontation and he had to be cautious.

As he got closer, he heard the man shouting at the sky. "Come out now, little girl, or I will kill your mama!"

Penny looked terrified and he prayed Missy wouldn't fall for the bait. She was much safer wherever she was hiding and he hoped she stayed there.

"Call her," the man shouted at Penny, pressing the gun against her once again.

"I won't do it," she responded.

Good. This guy wasn't going to ever get Penny to lure her daughter to her death. Caleb knew her better than to think she would ever do that. And, if Stafford couldn't get to Missy, he was going to fail in his mission. But, on a closer look, Penny was indeed pale and he spotted blood on her shirt. She'd been shot and was bleeding. From the looks of her, she wouldn't be able to stand much longer.

Stafford grunted in frustration at his inability to get

her to do his bidding. He knocked her to the ground. Caleb's gut clenched and he nearly fired, but Stafford still had the advantage with the gun. He aimed at her. "I said call her out now or I will shoot you."

"No," she cried. So Stafford pressed the gun to her head.

It was time to grab Stafford's attention before he lost his patience and took the lethal shot. It was time to end this. Caleb glanced across the field at Luke and gave him the signal that he was about to engage. He knew his cousin would want to wait for backup but he wasn't close enough to see the fire in Stafford's face. Caleb was. Stafford was spiraling and that meant Penny's life was in real danger with no time to wait. Stafford was on the verge of snapping if Penny didn't do as he wanted. And she wouldn't. He knew that about her. She would protect her daughter with her last dying breath.

Caleb couldn't let it reach that. He had to act before this maniac took everything from him.

Hot tears spilled down her face. She couldn't hold them back. The combination of fear and pain and weakness from loss of blood was beginning to take its toll. She didn't know how much longer she could hold on but the longer she did, the better Missy's chance of living. She prayed her daughter was holed up somewhere, hidden well from Stafford.

Yes, she'd prayed. The truth had hit her like a ton of bricks the moment Stafford had shot her. She was going to die and God was the only one who could save her daughter. She might have given up on Him, but He'd never given up on her. He'd led them here to Jessup, Texas, and to Caleb.

Caleb.

She prayed he knew how much she loved him. She would never have the opportunity to tell him now. But he would be there for Missy. She was certain he would make sure her daughter was protected and safe. He would fight for Missy just as he'd fought for her.

Stafford pressed the gun to her head again and reissued his demand. "Call for her now!" he shouted. The gun was hard and cold against her cheek and his tone was splintered. He was about to lose his cool and kill her. She didn't want to die but she would never, ever, give up on ensuring her daughter's safety. Nothing he could do would entice her to lure Missy from wherever she was hiding.

"Let her go." Caleb stepped from behind an old tractor, gun raised and trained on Stafford.

Her heart leapt and hope swept through her. He'd come for them!

But she felt Stafford's demeanor change the moment he saw Caleb. He yanked Penny to her feet, making her cry out in pain from her gun wound. He dug the gun tighter against her. "Stay back or I'll shoot her."

"You don't want to do that, Stafford."

He stiffened in shock at Caleb's use of his name. She heard his breathing grow heavy.

"That's right. We know who you are and we know what you did. You were part of the bank robbery. Your sister gave you up. You shot and killed a federal agent.

Missy knew it and now everyone else does too. It's too late for you."

His gaze darted back and forth as if he were a caged animal looking for a way out.

Penny glanced at Caleb. His body was tense and his jaw clenched. Outwardly, he was calm and focused on the task at hand but she caught his eye momentarily when he looked her way and she thought she saw fear flicker in his green eyes. He was scared for her, scared of losing her.

Luke suddenly appeared from the other side, his gun raised and aimed at Stafford who turned, pulling her with him to warn him away.

"Stay back," he shouted at Luke who didn't move an inch.

This was now a showdown. They would take Stafford down before he could get to Missy, which she was thankful for. Only, she was also certain that Stafford was going to take her down with him.

Another figure appeared from behind the old tractor. Ed, the ranch manager. He held a rifle toward Stafford as several of the ranch hands followed behind him, all armed as well. "You're surrounded now. You won't get away."

Caleb grabbed Stafford's attention back to himself as sirens sounded in the distance. Lights were visible, turning off the road. "Our backup just arrived. There's no way out of this. Let the woman go and surrender."

Stafford was cornered and he knew it. Penny could feel his breath heave. She also knew that was when predators could be the most dangerous.

Caleb gripped his gun tighter and shouted at Stafford again. "I said let her go. Now!"

Stafford pulled her with him as he backed up, looking for his opening to escape or at least do some damage on his way out. "I'm not going to jail," he said as Caleb approached him. "I'm not going to jail."

He raised the gun to her head and she heard the click of the trigger. This was the end for her.

"No!" Caleb screamed, firing.

The blasts from the gun were deafening. Penny screamed too as she fell, her legs buckling under her as she tumbled to the ground along with Stafford whose arm still gripped her against him.

They hit dirt with a thud and his grip loosened. She pulled herself away but her body protested any movement.

Someone grabbed her arm and she screamed again.

"Penny, it's me. It's Caleb." The next moment, he was pulling her tightly into his embrace. His tone was full of gut-wrenching anguish when he spoke again. "I thought I'd lost you."

She glanced over his shoulder and spotted Stafford on the ground, inches away. Luke rushed toward him, holding the gun to him as he approached, just in case the man was playing possum. She saw Luke holster his weapon, a sign that Stafford wasn't getting back up. Stu Stafford was dead and, somehow, Penny was still alive.

"What happened?" she asked, confused. "He fired. I know he fired. I should be dead."

He pushed his hand through her hair. "You nearly were. My first shot knocked him backward, causing his shot to go high over your head. The next shot killed him."

He dropped the gun and pulled Penny into a full embrace. He kissed her face, then her lips as relief flooded her. "I was so scared," she admitted.

"I'm sorry I wasn't here for you."

"I knew you'd come." She smiled up at him but a whimper of pain seeped through.

He glanced at the wound on her side and his jaw tensed. It was bad and she knew it. She'd lost a lot of blood and being toted around by Stafford hadn't helped.

Sirens sounded and moments later, the pasture was full of police cars and an ambulance. "Over here! She needs help," Caleb called to the paramedics. He held her hand as they began to poke and prod her wound.

"How is she?" Caleb asked them.

The paramedic glanced up. "Looks like the bullet just grazed her side. She's lost a lot of blood and we need to get her to the hospital, but I think she's going to be okay."

Relief flooded her. She wasn't going to die. She might actually have a chance at life again. A life with Caleb. She stole a glance up at him and saw the same relief on his face. "Is it— Is it over?" Trepidation filled her question. With Stafford dead, would anyone else be coming after them?

He nodded and kissed her again. "It's over. He was the ringleader of the bank robbers. We believe he planned everything and was the one who hired men to hunt you both down. He even had the child psychologist plant a tracker in Missy's toy monkey."

"Dr. Williams?"

He nodded. "She's his half-sister, and he threatened her family to get her to cooperate. He was behind everything. With him dead, you're safe now. We can tie him to the ring, which means we have them all as accessories to assault, murder and witness tampering as well as bank robbery. They're going away for a long time. We'll find the men they hired to come after you. Then you and Missy will be safe."

Hope filled her. "Does that mean we don't have to go into witness protection? We can stay?" The idea of not having to leave Caleb, of being able to remain at Harmon Ranch and have a future, was almost more than she could hope for.

He laughed, then squeezed her hand. "Well, this isn't exactly the most romantic moment, but yes, you and Missy can stay. I *want* you to stay, Penny. I love you. I want to marry you and make a family with you and Missy if you'll have me."

Her heart soared at his sweet request. It was everything she wanted too. "I love you too, Caleb. Yes, I'll marry you."

"I want to be part of your and Missy's family." He stopped, then pulled away from her. "Wait a minute. Where is she? Where is Missy?"

Penny's expression tightened as she realized they'd been so caught up in relief that the ordeal was over that they hadn't found Missy yet.

She started to stand, only to have the paramedic try to stop her. "You shouldn't move, ma'am. We need to get you to the hospital to have your wound seen about."

"I have to find my daughter." Caleb took her hand

and helped her to her feet. She called out for her. "Missy, it's okay, honey. You can come out now. Everything is fine."

Caleb joined in. "Missy. Come on out. You're safe now." He turned to look at her. "You really have no idea where she is?"

"No. I told her to run and hide. I don't know where she went."

She should have come out at the sound of Penny's voice. Suddenly all the terrible things that could happen to a small child on a ranch flooded her brain. *Oh, God, please let her be okay.* She knew Stafford hadn't gotten to her, but could something else terrible have happened while she was racing to get away from him?

Luke and Ed and the ranch hands and officers joined in the search, spreading out and calling for Missy.

"I'm sure she's fine," Caleb assured her. "She's just doing what she was told to do—hiding. We will find her."

Suddenly, a small figure appeared, crawling through the opening in the old hideout. Before she could holler, Caleb called out to her. "Missy, it's okay. You're safe now."

Relief flooded Penny. She longed to jump up and run to her daughter but she wasn't able to. She called to her instead. "Missy!" The girl darted toward them and fell into her arms. "Are you okay?" she asked, checking her over.

"I'm okay. I did what you said. I ran and hid in the fort. He didn't find me there. Did I do okay?"

Penny brushed her hair from her face and hugged her again. "Yes, baby. You did great."

Caleb hugged them both, then led Penny back to the paramedics to finish getting herself fixed up. As she watched him with Missy, she knew they'd finally made it. With God's help and Caleb's, they'd survived this ordeal.

Caleb watched as the paramedics loaded Penny into the ambulance. She'd given him quite the fright but it looked like she was going to be okay.

They were all going to be okay now that Stafford was dead and the others in the ring would be held accountable. No one else was going to get to Penny or Missy, not as long as he could help it.

He scooped Missy up into a hug and she wrapped her arms around his neck. "I love you," Missy whispered, and the joy he felt at those simple words was only eclipsed by her mother's declaration of love a moment earlier.

He had the two most important people in his life with him now and he wasn't ever letting them go again.

"You know, we could get some LED lights and string them up inside the fort. Maybe get some pillows and toys. It could be a proper girls' fort."

Her eyes lit up at his suggestion, then she looked to her mother inside the ambulance. "Can we, Mama? Can we? Are we staying here at the ranch?"

Penny reached for her hand and she and Caleb climbed inside and sat beside her. "Caleb has asked us to stay. Would you like that, Missy?"

She clapped her hands. "Yes, yes, yes. I want to live here." She turned to Caleb and hugged him. "I never want to leave."

He laughed and kissed her cheek. "You never have to, sweetheart." He pulled Penny into his arms and kissed her too.

He'd finally found his forever family and he was never letting them go again.

# EPILOGUE

Caleb watched from the front window as Missy played in the yard with Luke's kids, Kenzie and Dustin. Her squeals of laughter made his heart happy.

Luke had decided to take that job with Brett's security firm in Dallas and his family was enjoying their last few days at Harmon Ranch before their new adventure. The house should feel empty again with the family leaving, but it didn't. Not since Penny and Missy had moved in permanently. He and Penny had gotten married in a small, intimate ceremony two months earlier. They'd wanted something different but had chosen to go for something simple when it looked like she and Missy might have to enter witness protection after all. He'd been determined to give up everything and go with them. He wasn't letting them leave without him, not when they'd finally found happiness. Now that the danger had passed, he didn't regret it. Marrying her in any form or fashion had been worth it.

He'd just ended a call with Agent Sinclair and gotten word that, after months of negotiations, all the men involved in the bank robbery—plus the men Stafford had hired to kill Penny and Missy—had pled guilty. There would be no need for Missy to testify against anyone. It was over. She was safe and they could finally put this nightmare behind them.

Penny walked to the window and stood beside him. A smile spread across her face as she saw how her daughter had blossomed since coming to Harmon Ranch. They'd found her a good therapist and she was working through the trauma she'd endured.

He slid his arm around Penny. She was healing nicely too.

He noticed something in her hand. "What's that?"

She held up a folded sheet of paper. "This is Missy's latest drawing."

He groaned and braced himself. Ending the danger against her hadn't completely ended her morbid drawings. They weren't nearly as common now but they still happened.

He unfolded it, only to find that, to his surprise, it wasn't the dark image he'd expected to see. She'd drawn a picture of a family. The woman was obviously Penny. Missy had written the word *Mama* over her and *Daddy* over the man. Over the child, she'd written the word *Missy*.

He zeroed in on something in the woman's hands. "What is that?"

She smiled. "I think that's supposed to be a baby."

A rush of satisfaction flowed over him. "I love that she's thinking about a happy future."

"So do I. I never thought we would get to this place, Caleb. I never thought we could be this happy."

He hugged her, then had a great idea. "What do you say we give her that baby brother or sister she drew in the picture?"

She blinked back tears at his suggestion. "I think that's a wonderful idea." She kissed him, then grinned mischievously. "I hope you don't change your mind, because it's too late to take it back."

"Take what back?"

Her eyes sparkled with the news. "The baby."

A wave of joy rushed through him. He touched her stomach in awe. "Are you telling me that we're having a baby?"

She nodded. "Are you happy?"

"I'm thrilled." He pulled her into his arms and kissed her.

God had truly blessed him with so much. A wife, a daughter and now a new baby. The future was bright and Harmon Ranch was finally a home.

\* \* \* \* \*

*If you enjoyed this Cowboy Protectors novel,*
*be sure to pick up the previous books in this series*
*by Virginia Vaughan:*

Kidnapped in Texas
Texas Ranch Target

*Available now from Love Inspired Suspense!*

Dear Reader,

The past few months, my life has been turned upside down by multiple unexpected situations. None of these were life-threatening events but they sure left me feeling overwhelmed and weary. As I was rereading this story, I was reminded that God is in control, even when life gets hectic—like mine—or dangerous—like Penny and Missy's. I hope you too found this reminder hidden in the pages of this story.

I hope you enjoyed getting to know Caleb and Penny. I look forward to meeting and learning about cousin Tucker in the next and final book of my Cowboy Protectors series. I hope you'll join me.

I love to hear from my readers! Please keep in touch. You can reach me online at my website www.virginia-vaughanonline.com or follow me on Facebook at www.Facebook.com/ginvaughanbooks.

Blessings!
*Virginia*

# Get 3 FREE REWARDS!

## We'll send you 2 FREE Books plus a FREE Mystery Gift.

Both the **Love Inspired**® and **Love Inspired**® Suspense series feature compelling novels filled with inspirational romance, faith, forgiveness and hope.

---

**YES!** Please send me 2 FREE novels from the Love Inspired or Love Inspired Suspense series and my FREE gift (gift is worth about $10 retail). After receiving them, if I don't wish to receive any more books, I can return the shipping statement marked "cancel." If I don't cancel, I will receive 6 brand-new Love Inspired Larger-Print books or Love Inspired Suspense Larger-Print books every month and be billed just $6.49 each in the U.S. or $6.74 each in Canada. That is a savings of at least 16% off the cover price. It's quite a bargain! Shipping and handling is just 50¢ per book in the U.S. and $1.25 per book in Canada.* I understand that accepting the 2 free books and gift places me under no obligation to buy anything. I can always return a shipment and cancel at any time by calling the number below. The free books and gift are mine to keep no matter what I decide.

Choose one:  ☐ **Love Inspired**        ☐ **Love Inspired**        ☐ **Or Try Both!**
               **Larger-Print**           **Suspense**               (122/322 & 107/307
               (122/322 BPA GRPA)         **Larger-Print**           BPA GRRP)
                                          (107/307 BPA GRPA)

Name (please print)

Address                                                                      Apt. #

City                            State/Province                    Zip/Postal Code

**Email:** Please check this box ☐ if you would like to receive newsletters and promotional emails from Harlequin Enterprises ULC and its affiliates. You can unsubscribe anytime.

---

Mail to the **Harlequin Reader Service:**
**IN U.S.A.:** P.O. Box 1341, Buffalo, NY 14240-8531
**IN CANADA:** P.O. Box 603, Fort Erie, Ontario L2A 5X3

**Want to try 2 free books from another series?** Call 1-800-873-8635 or visit www.ReaderService.com.

---

*Terms and prices subject to change without notice. Prices do not include sales taxes, which will be charged (if applicable) based on your state or country of residence. Canadian residents will be charged applicable taxes. Offer not valid in Quebec. This offer is limited to one order per household. Books received may not be as shown. Not valid for current subscribers to the Love Inspired or Love Inspired Suspense series. All orders subject to approval. Credit or debit balances in a customer's account(s) may be offset by any other outstanding balance owed by or to the customer. Please allow 4 to 6 weeks for delivery. Offer available while quantities last.

**Your Privacy**—Your information is being collected by Harlequin Enterprises ULC, operating as Harlequin Reader Service. For a complete summary of the information we collect, how we use this information and to whom it is disclosed, please visit our privacy notice located at corporate.harlequin.com/privacy-notice. From time to time we may also exchange your personal information with reputable third parties. If you wish to opt out of this sharing of your personal information, please visit readerservice.com/consumerchoice or call 1-800-873-8635. **Notice to California Residents**—Under California law, you have specific rights to control and access your data. For more information on these rights and how to exercise them, visit corporate.harlequin.com/california-privacy.

LIRLIS23